Katie Ward

Katie Ward always knew that she wanted to write for a living. After completing a degree in Journalism at the University for the Creative Arts in Farnham, she moved to Dublin. While there, she had a short story published in an anthology titled *Do the Write Thing* which was part of a competition being run by Irish TV show *Seoige and O'Shea*. This story was originally written when Katie was 14 after she was inspired by an article in her favourite teen magazine. The anthology reached the Irish Bestsellers List. Katie was also shortlisted for a competition judged by Man Booker Prize-winning author Roddy Doyle a few months later.

Katie currently lives in Devon where she sings in a community choir and has recently taken up archery.

The Pretender is her first Young Adult novel.

The Pretender

THE PRETENDER

Katie Ward

The Pretender

A CIP catalogue for this book is available from The British Library

ISBN e-book
978-1-9164300-1-3

ISBN paperback
978-1-9164300-0-6

Typeset by movedesign.co.uk
Printed and bound in Great Britain by
Kindle Direct Publishing

This book is dedicated to my mother, Catherine Ward and to all my family and friends who have given me their wholehearted support and who have always believed in me. A special thank you to my late, Great-Aunt Maggie-Anne, for introducing me to the original book all those years ago.

Dear Reader,

The Pretender is an adaptation of Mark Twain's novel T*he Prince and the Pauper*. Twain's story sees King Henry VIII's son, Prince Edward, accidentally switch places with abused beggar-boy Tom Canty, when the boys curiously swap clothes.

I first read this story when I was 10 years old on the journey home after spending the summer in Scotland with my family. While I loved it, I disliked the original ending. So, I decided to modernise it and create an ending better suited to such a great story.

Instead of the House of Tudor, I've resurrected the French Monarchy which was abolished in 1792. I have also created an imaginary Royal Family for Switzerland.

The Pretender is set in the present day and juxtaposes the opulent life of Princess Isabella with the deprivation experienced by Sophia. When the two girls decide to trade their two very different worlds, neither of them realise just what they've let themselves in for…

Katie Ward

The 'Pretender' comes from the term "Pretender to the Throne" which is used to describe someone who lays claim to an abolished throne…or a throne already occupied by another.

The Pretender

Chapter 1

The town of Fontainebleau near Paris, June 2005

The blackness of the night has always been a comfort, concealing me from the dangers of the light. I awaken when the familiar sounds fill my ears - the heavy footsteps of my father, the crash of whatever has got in his way falling to the floor, and the door slamming as my mother makes herself scarce . . . Goose-bumps rise upon my skinny arms. Trembling, I hug my comforter, my 'binkie', to my chest tightly. I'm supposed to be brave now I'm five years old.

'Sophia, hide - quickly!' My older sister Mireille feverishly pushes me into the one hiding place our father has yet to find, the narrow space between the wardrobe and the wall, before jumping back into bed and pretending to be fast asleep.

Suddenly, the veil of darkness is pierced by the harsh overhead light, exposing everything it touches to the vision of our father.

'Where is she? Where is the little witch?' I listen to his menacing words from where I'm huddled, too afraid to move, fearing each breath I take will reveal where I am. I see him storm over to my sister, angry at her lack of response.

'Father, I don't know where she is - she was in bed asleep. I've just woken up.' My sister's voice is trembling.

'Don't lie to me. I know you protect her. The minute that wretched child was born, you've defended her.' He loses his balance, stumbles for a moment, then rights himself, hissing at her, 'Well, since I can't find her, I'll just make do with you.'

'Please don't hurt me, Father. Please don't hurt me!'

I watch, petrified, clutching my binkie as our father grabs Mireille by the hair, dragging her onto the floor before kicking her hard in the stomach with his right foot.

'Get up, you little wimp,' he slurs. 'Get up or I'll kill you right here. Is that what you want, Mireille? Who will protect your precious Sophia when you're dead?'

Mireille pulls herself up from the floor, her legs barely able to support her own weight.

Smiling cruelly, my father waits until she is standing in front of him, pain etched across her face. Then, without warning, he punches her in the face, causing her to topple backwards onto the bed, sobbing and holding her bloodied nose.

Swaying, he nearly falls over again, but steadies himself and chuckles. 'Your turn tomorrow, Sophia,' he utters, then his voice hardens. 'You can't hide for ever. You can't outsmart me, you little brat.'

The veil of darkness falls once again as our father lurches out of the room, leaving a lingering stench of whisky behind him. A few moments later, after I hear his bedroom door close, I squeeze out of my hiding place and tiptoe over to where Mireille is lying coiled up. Taking my binkie, I gently hold it against her bleeding nose. Then, lying down next to her, I wrap my small arms around her. Together we cry . . .

Notre Dame Boarding School, Chartres, June 2018

Sitting bolt upright in bed, my heart races and terror courses through my body. I left that life when I was seven years old yet the nightmares persist. Every night, I see my sister's face, remember how much she did to save me from *him* and how much she loved me, and I pray she is ok. My dearest Mireille, even at eleven years old she was more of a mother to me than our own mother could ever be.

And then it dawns on me what day it is. The day that will pull me from the safety of my boarding school here in Chartres and place me back with the family I thought I'd left behind in Fontainebleau.

Pulling open the curtains, the warmth of the sun caresses my face. I close my eyes and brace myself to accept that today is my eighteenth birthday. Turning to look in the mirror, my brown eyes are red and tired while my olive complexion looks pale adding to my drained look. Reaching for my brush, I gently comb the tangles out of my long dark hair.

'Happy birthday to you, Happy birthday to you, Happy birthday, dear Sophia, Happy birthday to you!' My three closest friends Mai, Julienne and Rosalie bundle excitedly into my room, still dressed in their pjs and dressing-gowns, as they flop down on my bed.

'Thank you,' I tell them. 'I never expected you all to get up this early just for me.'

'Soph, it's your eighteenth birthday, we were always going to make it special for you,' Mai says. 'Besides, you're the first of us to officially become an adult. Not to mention the fact that you share your birthday with Princess Isabella.

Perhaps you're her long-lost twin and the nurses got you mixed up at the hospital?' she teases. 'These things happen all the time.'

'Mai, I hate to burst your bubble, but we were born in different hospitals. We also come from very different worlds. Princess Isabella was born into a life of plenty and prestige - but most of all into a family who love her. As for me, I'm pretty sure I was the only seven year old who looked forward to going to boarding school because it meant I would finally be safe.'

Thinking of the home to which I must soon return, I shudder.

'*Safe*?!' Julienne says. 'What was wrong - and why have you never spoken of this before?'

Concern flickers across my friends' faces as they await my reply. Thinking back to my dream last night, the dread still fresh in my mind, at long last I find the courage to open up about my past.

'I've never told anyone this before, but my father used to beat me - a lot. He and my mother are addicts, you see.' I feel my cheeks redden with shame but I know I must continue. 'One of my earliest memories is seeing the purple bruises through my school shirt in the mirror. I remember feeling so ashamed because I actually thought I deserved the punishment. I believed I was a bad person, like he always told me. I was so scared that people would find out how terrible I was that I spoke to no one.'

I stop to swallow before going on. 'It was my English teacher at Kindergarten, Miss Shaw who first noticed the bruises. She immediately reported it to the authorities. I know she wanted to help me but my father is very charming and believable when he wants to be. The outcome was that the social worker was tricked into believing that I was being bullied at school, not at home.

'The social worker who came to see us was barely out of the house when he attacked me again . . . but this time he went further than he ever had before, burning me with a lit cigarette. I'll never forget the sound and smell of it sizzling through my skin.'

As my friend's gasp with shock, I feel tears sliding down my face, but it is too late to stop now. I have to tell them everything.

'He told me it was my punishment for trying to get him into trouble. To this day, I remember the look of satisfaction on his face when that social worker left. It was clear he felt untouchable.'

Aghast, the others fall silent as they try to comprehend what I've just told them.

Finally, my closest friend Mai says gently, 'Oh dear God, Soph, I can't believe you never told us all this before. I'll never forget how good you were when I was being bullied by those girls who kept telling me I should go back to Vietnam, despite me being born in France.'

'We had no idea that it had been so tough for you,' Mai continues clearly appalled, I see the others both nod in agreement as she adds 'So, how did you get out?'

'I was five years old when he burnt me,' I say quietly.

'But none of us started here until we were seven years old!' Julienne cries. 'You can't have had to endure living at home for two more years?'

'There was no choice for me, I had to stay there. The violence continued but not as bad as before. Miss Shaw and I never talked about it after that; it just became an unspoken reality. The bruises told their own story. I was a bright girl though, and that's how Miss Shaw helped to keep me safe. Every day after school I stayed behind for as long as I could. We would always walk back to the house together. Then when I turned six, she suggested applying for a scholarship to boarding school to remove me from my home once and for all. At first, I was worried about leaving my sister Mireille, but for the first time in my life, I felt hopeful. I do have another sister Manon but we were never close, I couldn't trust her so I always kept my distance, as I did with my mother.'

'As strange as it sounds, I enjoyed the extra lessons. Even though the other kids were eager to get out and play after school, I didn't mind staying behind to practice my writing, do sums or learn spellings. Unlike them, I didn't want to go home. It scared me to walk back into that house never knowing whether I'd get attacked or whether it would be Mireille or Manon's turn this time. It was usually me though who got the brunt of is anger - I still have no idea why - and the only reason Mireille got it so bad was because she looked out for me.' Without me in the house, I hoped that it would be easier for everyone.

'When Miss Shaw told me, I'd been accepted at Notre Dame. It was the best news I've ever had!' I admit shyly, 'When I first saw a picture of this place, it looked so grand I thought it was a palace. I remember being terrified that my father would say no, but Miss Shaw promised me he wouldn't. In her, my father had met his match - which just makes me love her even more.'

I turn to my friends and say impulsively, 'It sounds weird, but I've always felt an affinity with Cinderella. We were both let down by those who were meant to care for us, but in Miss Shaw I too met my fairy godmother. She saved my life. Not a day goes by when I don't miss her and her lovely accent. It almost made me want to be British,' I say 'but I don't think I'd like the food.'

'Don't say that!' exclaims Mai. 'I wasn't going to say anything yet but I'm hoping to go to Oxford University. I've done so well in my Baccalaureate and I've just taken their entrance exam. I know the competition is fierce but I know I've got what it takes. Is Miss Shaw the lady you used to stay with during the holidays?'

'Yes, that's right. On the day she drove me here, she promised that I would never have to go back to my family. When I think that it's been a year now since her death, it makes me so sad. I just wish it was him that was taken, not her. It's so unfair!' I exclaim.

Turning to give Mai a hug, I tell her: 'Mai, you're the cleverest person I know and you will make the most amazing doctor. It'll be their loss if they don't take you at Oxford, but there are plenty of other good places to study medicine in the UK.' I see Rosalie and Julienne nod their approval as they each come to give Mai a hug too.

'Thanks, Soph. I will keep my options open as the research I've done into Oxford does show a disproportionality with ethnic minority groups being accepted – unless of course they are mega-rich. But you know if they can't see past my race then that's their issue, not mine.'

Mai takes my hand as concern again etches itself upon her face. 'Look, Soph, if your teacher didn't want you to go back, then don't. You're more than welcome to live with us in Versailles. My parents adore you and it's not like we don't have enough space in the house. We have rooms we don't even know what to do with, so you'd be doing us a favour. Please come home with me.'

'Thank you,' I say with sincerity. 'Your family has always been so good to me. But if I'm honest, I think the time has come for me to confront my family. If I don't, then I'll always be afraid of my him. I want to make peace with my past so that I'm able to move on. Even if Miss Shaw was still alive, this day was always going to come, and deep down I've always known that. In three weeks' time, when term ends, I have to go back and face my family.'

'I know you do Soph, but just remember that we'll always be here for you no matter what,' Julienne gently consoles, being closely followed by Rosalie who also pledges her support.

'Yes,' Mai says. 'If you need help, I'm always just a phone call away. Besides, my dad is Police Commissioner, so the days of your father getting away with throwing his fists around are over.' Her tone softens. 'Well, while you may have to face your past soon, today is all about celebrating your birthday. Now, what's a birthday without presents? This one's from me.'

She hands me a small box wrapped in cobalt-blue paper with a contrasting bright pink bow.

'Did you wrap this yourself?' I ask. 'It looks too nice to open. I'll try not to tear the paper.' I try to gently peel away the tape from the parcel.

'Don't be soft, just rip it open.'

Unwrapping the paper, I look down to see an iPhone 8. I stare at the box in disbelief, astounded by Mai's generosity.

'Soph,' she says, 'you're my best friend and you've made the past eleven years the best of my life. I'll never forget the kindness you showed me in those first days - the way you stood up to those bullies and their taunts. I'd lost hope of anyone accepting me but you proved me wrong; you have always supported and protected me. So, this is my way of showing you that no matter where you are, you'll always be able to contact me. You know how much my folks love you? Well, they're happy to take care of the bill so it'll never cost you a penny.'

Whilst I may not have had much luck with the family I was born into, I've certainly hit the jackpot when it comes to my friends. Reaching over to hug them one by one, I feel so grateful that our paths crossed all those years ago.

'I just don't know what I'm going to do without you all,' I say huskily, 'because I think of you all more as my family than my actual family.'

'Don't say that, Sophia, or you'll make us all cry. We'll stay in contact and find a way to see each other so nothing has to change, not really. This is from me and Julienne.' Rosalie hands me a small polka-dot gift-wrapped box.

'Thank you both so much, I can't wait to find out what it is.' I unwrap the gift to reveal a small, pale-blue box with an emblematic white bow tied neatly at the top.

'A Tiffany box - I have a Tiffany box!' My voice squeaks with excitement as emotion pricks the back of my eyes.

Opening the box, I look down to see an exquisite heart-shaped necklace. I lift it out and it spins around on its silver chain, sparkling in the sunshine as I raise it in front of my face.

'It's a locket,' Rosalie says. 'Open it up and see what's inside.'

I do so carefully, scared that I'll break it. Inside are two photos. One of us all together and one of just me and Mai.

'It's so beautiful,' I proclaim. 'It's never going to leave my neck, I'll treasure it forever.'

I place my oversized birthday card, displaying a huge '18' written on it, on the shelf next to my bed. Now I'm ready to reveal the surprises I have for *them*.

'Thank you all so much for your thoughtful and beautiful gifts,' I say, then announce: 'I wish I could be there on your birthdays too, if my situation was different you know I would be– so it just means that you'll all have to open your presents now.'

Opening the cupboard, I hand out long flat boxes to Mai, Rosalie and Julienne. My hands tremble slightly as I watch them pull out a dress from each of their boxes.

'Wow, Soph, I absolutely love it. Where did you get it? I've never seen a dress like this before.' Mai gushes as she examines her dress.

'I didn't *buy* these dresses for you,' I explain shyly. 'I designed them and then made them for you myself. Each one is unique: no one else will ever have one the same.'

While I've made my own clothes for years – it came from necessity and something I've never discussed as it's not easy to admit that you don't have enough money to buy your own clothes - so it feels strange to now be making an outfit for someone else. By offering these dresses it feels as if I'm exposing a part of me that has never been seen before, and this makes me feel uncomfortable.

'Sophia, it's perfect. Just you wait until people see me in this at my party- they'll all be wanting you to make them one.' Rosalie holds the dress up to herself in front of the mirror, admiring how it looks against her.

'Amen to that. I can scarcely believe you made these with your own hands. I now own a Sophia Lazarus original. Wow. You're so talented.' Julienne gently strokes the material before folding her dress back into the box. 'Even though you can't be with us in person, when I wear this dress it'll feel like you are there. I love that because you'll be so missed.'

'You'd better Instagram me the pictures,' I reply. 'I can't wait to see you all wearing your dresses, all made-up and with the right jewellery and shoes. You'll look beautiful.'

Three heads nod back silently, all still engrossed in their new dresses.

'Right, we need to go and get ready,' Mai says, her bossiness making us smile. 'We have a day of fun planned for you, Sophia, starting with a birthday brunch in that restaurant you've always wanted to try. While you may not be an actual Princess, we'll certainly make you feel like one today.'

As my friends race back to their rooms to get ready, my mind wanders to what will happen in three weeks' time when the school term ends and this part of my life comes to a close; when the nightmare I thought I had escaped eleven years ago will once again become my reality.

Like every year, my thoughts turn to what Princess Isabella might be doing for her birthday. Is any part of her day like mine? Is it only a birthday that we share - or has the synchronicity of our births left us both more alike than we realise?

Chapter 2

Château de Fontainebleau, June 2018

Tonight, I'll be attending my first ever ball, which is being held in honour of my eighteenth birthday. For years my pleas to be allowed to attend a ball fell on deaf ears, my father King Henri resolute that these occasions were no place for a child. Although I note that his stance has relaxed since then, for my two younger sisters will be joining us tonight.

Picking up the hem of my ball gown, I twirl slowly in front of my bedroom mirror, watching the rich scarlet satin as it glimmers. Delicately tracing the crystals on the bodice with my fingers, I pull my hair off my face, holding it with one hand while I try to style the rest with the other. The contrast of the red against my olive skin and chocolate-brown hair makes this the perfect dress.

There's a tap at the door before our housekeeper Celeste pops her head round, smiling as she says: 'Isabella, posing with your dress isn't going to make time pass any sooner. You'd be better off doing something useful instead.'

While she carries her cleaning stuff into my suite, I feel my face blush at the intrusion, although I know she is only teasing me.

'I just don't know what to do with myself right now,' I

say, taking the dress off with her help and putting my jeans back on. 'We've a million rooms in this palace yet there isn't one thing for me to do apart from count down the hours until the guests start arriving.' I collapse onto one of the chairs, Celeste frowns at me, making it clear I'm getting in her way.

'Well, Eddie's back from Paris putting the finishing touches to your birthday cake, so . . .'

'Celeste, are you serious? Eddie's making my birthday cake? What a lovely surprise.'

Eddie Laurent has lived at the cottage on the Palace estate with us since he was ten years old when his mother, Leonda, became our Head Chef. I remember fondly the stories she would tell us about what it was like for her growing up in Jamaica. Despite being 4 years younger than him, we quickly became playmates; our friendship the most enduring of my life and the one I treasure the most. Over a year ago, he moved to Paris to work in one of the country's finest patisserie's as a sugar artist. It surprises me how much I miss him when he's gone.

A stricken look crosses Celeste's face.

'I forgot I wasn't supposed to tell you! I just thought you'd like to see him, to stop you being bored.' She gives a tut of exasperation. 'Why have I never learned to think before I speak.'

'Don't worry,' I comfort her. 'No one will know you ever said a thing about it. Perhaps I'll go and stick my head around the door to the kitchens and see if I can "accidentally" bump into him. He'll surely have some stories of Paris to tell me, and about all the things he's been doing.'

'Right. Well off you run then, while I get on in here.'

Leaving Celeste, I skip along the landing, down the main staircase on my way to the basement kitchens. Halfway down, I spot my father speaking with Baptiste, our equerry. The two men are so engrossed in their conversation that they don't even notice me quietly slip across the foyer towards the back stairs.

Stopping just shy of the main door to the kitchens, I peep around it, trying to catch a glimpse of my cake.

'You never were any good at sneaking up on people, Isabella,' Eddie says coolly, without even turning around. 'You always think you are being so quiet, but to me you sound like a herd of baby elephants.'

'Eddie, what a surprise - I thought you were in Paris,' I lamely say as he turns towards me, his eyebrows furrow in disbelief.

'Really? Because I got the distinct impression you were sneaking up on me just now to see what I'm doing. And you knew very well that I was coming - as if I'd miss your eighteenth-birthday celebration.'

'OK fine, I'll admit it: Celeste let slip that you were making my birthday cake but I swore to her that I would still act surprised. So, I might have been trying to get a glimpse of it for myself.'

'Hard luck, Isabella. I finished decorating it yesterday and it's been put in a safe place away from prying eyes. We want it to be a big surprise for tonight. Right now, I'm just getting prepped for tonight before the caterers turn up.'

'I've an idea,' I say. 'What if I only look at it with one eye open? Then I won't be able to see it properly and it'll still be a surprise. You can't deny it, Eddie - I'm a genius!'

His handsome face creases into a smile as he runs his hands through his short dark hair. Looking at my friend,

I notice how tall he is now, there never used to be much difference when we were kids but now he towers above me. His shoulders seem broader than when I last saw him too, I swear each time he returns from Paris I notice something different about him.

'You're the most impatient girl I've ever known. But it's true that I'd like to see your reaction, especially after all the hard work I've put in. So, OK - but just don't go thinking you've charmed me.'

I follow Eddie into one of the walk-in larders, eager to see the cake in all its glory.

Upon a heavy silver base stands an eight-tier cake, each tier descending to create an elegant shape. Lifelike roses piped in pink, white and purple fall down the side of the cake, giving the illusion of growth. Strategically placed in the centre of each rose are diamanté decorations that sparkle in the light, making it seem as if the entire cake is in fact made of diamonds. Scattered amongst the flowers are an array of delicate butterflies, poised to fly off at any moment.

I am speechless.

'Do you like it?' Eddie looks anxious. And when I still say nothing, he rushes on: 'I was inspired by your love of butterflies as a child. Do you remember how many times you asked me to catch one for you?' He reminisces ruefully, 'I was never very good at that: I was always too afraid of hurting them.'

'Me, too.' At last I find my voice. 'When did you ever see me catch a single butterfly, Eddie?'

'Not once, now you mention it. What a pair we were.'

'I'm so pleased to have you back,' I tell him impulsively. 'I miss you when you're away in Paris. To have you make my cake is so special. I love it. Thank you.'

'I miss you too, Isabella. It only seems like yesterday when we were both kids running around playing hide-and-seek in the gardens. Now I'm away in Paris being mentored in sugar artistry and designing the most exquisite cakes, and you're destined to become Queen.' He sighs. 'How did that happen? I don't feel equipped to be an adult yet. I still feel too young.'

'Don't remind me,' I say gloomily. 'I'd love to go to Paris and live in the real world too. Maybe I'm lucky to be a Princess but I don't want to be Queen. My life will never be mine; everything I do is controlled and orchestrated and it always will be. It's like I'm a puppet on a string moving to the wishes of my master. How can this be my kingdom when I'm not even allowed out of the palace grounds without someone's permission?'

Eddie and I move out of the larder, and he closes the door behind us.

'I can't just be normal,' I say heatedly. 'I can't go out shopping, go to the cinema or travel on a public train or do any ordinary things like that. I just feel so trapped.' My voice rises in frustration causing Eddie to look and check that no one can hear us.

'Hush!' he warns me. 'You're not trapped, Isabella, but you do have to live within the constraints of your royal life - and the sooner you come to terms with that, the better.'

'Can't you persuade my father to let me come and visit you in Paris?' I ask.

'Are you joking?' Eddie goes to the big fridge, takes out some mango juice and pours us both a glass, before searching the cupboards and returning with my favourite chocolate sables. 'When have I ever been able to persuade your father of anything? When have you, for that matter?'

'Point taken. Thanks.' I take a long drink of the cool juice, then grumble, 'I suppose I'm just destined to live half a life and to never know the world outside my window.' My voice becomes choked. 'Will I ever leave Fontainebleau?'

'Now you're just being melodramatic,' Eddie says briskly, taking our empty glasses and placing them into one of the dishwashers. 'You've left Fontainebleau plenty of times, so don't exaggerate. Face it - no one's life is free from constraint, and even if you were born into the lowliest of families you wouldn't have the freedom you think you would. Believe me, freedom is just an illusion. If you keep chasing freedom like this, it'll only lead to trouble.'

'Trouble is my middle name, it's what I do,' I reply stubbornly. 'Besides, you know it doesn't count when you go away with family. I want to leave here by myself - as an ordinary woman, *not* as a Princess.'

Picking up my hand and giving it a comforting squeeze, he speaks softly, 'Look at my mum. She was born to an ordinary family in Jamaica, then she moved to Paris to train in Raymond Blanc's kitchen. When my Dad died, she had to support us both on her own.

Eddie gestures at the four walls. 'Does she have more freedom than you? Is she not tied to her job here, which provides the money she needs to keep things going? The point I'm trying to make is that an ordinary life won't give you the freedom you crave. We are all tied to whatever provides our living, if we enjoy what we do it's just a bonus.' I watch thoughtfully as he arranges thin lemon and lime slices on a long silver dish which he puts into the fridge, along with a bowl of freshly chopped mint.

'Enjoy the life you have now and be satisfied, don't

waste time hankering after something that may not be all it's cracked up to be.' He glances at his watch. 'Right, I need to get on, or I'll be the one in trouble. The caterers will be here soon, and Mum and I need to have finished our parts.'

Just then, Leonda comes bustling in.

'Eddie, what you playing at? I left you to prep this an hour ago. Time is ticking on. Come on – everything has to be perfect. The caterers will be needing them soon.' Her musical accent makes her sound sterner than she is. 'And Isabella! What are you doing down here on your birthday?'

'I'm sorry, Leonda, it's my fault. I haven't seen Eddie for so long, we were just catching up on all the things he's been doing in Paris.'

'Well, precious, your father's looking for you. He's in his study so you'd better go to him and leave Eddie to finish up here.'

I look up at Leonda's kindly face; her beautiful dark skin is peppered with freckles across her nose and her hair is neatly combed back into a bun. Her radiating smile is infectious even when she is being stern. I wish I had been able to know Eddie's father too; while I know he was French I can't picture what he might have been like. I often wonder if Eddie is like him. I suspect he is.

I say my goodbyes and hurriedly make my way up to my father's study. The dark mahogany wood that adorns these walls match beautifully with his antique furniture and together with the warm lighting, makes this one of the nicest rooms in the palace.

'Ah, there you are,' he says absent-mindedly. 'I wanted to catch you before you disappear to preen yourself. I've got something for you.'

'Here you are, sir.' I watch as Baptiste passes my father a small but beautifully wrapped present.

Daddy takes my hand and places the present in it. 'My darling,' he says, 'I had this made for you by the jeweller who created your mother's engagement ring.'

I open the box to reveal a diamond and sapphire locket, the delicate detail is truly beautiful. Carefully I prise apart the two halves to see a photo of my parents on one side and one of me and my younger sisters – Alix and Grace - on the other.

'Oh Daddy, I can't wait to wear it tonight. It'll contrast beautifully with my dress. This is the best gift I've ever had.' I give him a big hug and kiss his cheek.

'Sir, could I remind you that your guests are due to start arriving in two hours' Baptiste murmurs tactfully.

'Good heavens, is it that time already? My father hoists himself up from his seat, as we both head off to our rooms.

As my make-up artist finishes packing up her stuff and gets ready to leave, the hairdresser adds the final touches to my hair with a quick spray to keep everything in place. My hair is styled into a pretty chignon with loose curls falling around my face. There is a knock on my door before my mother walks in. The women curtsy to her as she enters, before they both leave my room. Mama comes over to join me.

'Let me look at you, love,' she says. 'You look beautiful and so grown up. The necklace is stunning - did you know that your father designed it himself, just like he did with my engagement ring?'

'Yes. He's a dark horse, isn't he? I never thought of him as an artistic type.'

'True, he never ceases to surprise me. If I think back, when it comes to your father nothing has ever been as it seemed - but in the best of ways. Come on, sweetheart, we're nearly ready to go. Your sisters are very excited!'

As I descend the Grand Staircase with my family, ready to greet the guests at my party, I feel every inch the Princess I'm supposed to be. However, amongst all the fun and laughter I can't ignore the restless notion that's plagued me for years: that there's so much more to life than just being a bird imprisoned in this gilded cage.

The Pretender

Chapter 3

Three weeks later . . .

The clouds darken, blotting out the sun as the train dashes towards Fountainbleau. While it takes two and a half hours from Chartres, all to soon the train pulls into the station. A sense of foreboding fills me. Should I have gone to stay with Mai?

Once off the train, I instantly feel as if I'm back where I started. My heart quickens as I look down the platform and see my sister Mireille walking towards me. She's twenty-four now, yet I recognise her immediately. She must have recognised me too. After all these years, I wasn't sure that she would.

Emotion grips me as I prepare to reunite with the only person in my family who ever cared for me.

'Sophia, you're absolutely gorgeous - what's happened to my baby sister? I can't believe you're actually here, and all grown up. I've missed you so much.'

We wrap our arms around each other, holding on tight.

'I've missed you too,' I tell her. 'For so long I've wanted you to know how grateful I am for everything you did for me. You were the only one who ever looked out for me and I've never forgotten that. I've never forgotten *you*. I see you every night from the moment I close my eyes until the moment I open them.'

Tears fall down our cheeks. It's so sad that nothing can ever replace our lost years. The pain of such a long separation cuts deep; the realisation of how much we've missed is there with us on the cold platform.

'You don't need to thank me for anything,' Mireille tells me, holding on to me closely. 'It was Miss Shaw's idea - but I always knew that going away to school was the only way you'd ever be safe.' She flinches. 'That look on his face after the social worker left - it still chills me to the core. I don't think you would be alive if you had stayed. No matter how much he hurt you, no matter how young you were, he couldn't break your defiance, which enraged him. It made him target you above us all.'

'Mireille, you protected me when no one else would. I have never forgotten the night you hid me, and he beat you up instead. He could have really hurt you, kicking and punching you like that. Miss Shaw was the only person who ever stood up to our father, but she couldn't have done it without you.'

'You would have done the same for me. We're sisters, aren't we? Besides, we've always shared a special bond from the moment you were born, more so than with Manon, even though I practically raised her too. But why are you talking about Miss Shaw in the past tense? Surely you've kept in touch?'

'Did you not hear the news? She died last year. I just feel so lost without her. I thought it would have got easier by now, but it hasn't - sometimes it's worse.'

'Oh no, that's awful - I can't believe it! What happened?'

'She developed sepsis after contracting a virus, and by the time it was discovered it was too late. She just wasn't able to fight it. Her death was so sudden, I didn't even get to say goodbye. I'd do anything to have her back again.' I admit fiercely: 'I wish it was our father who died. I hate that he is allowed to live while a kind heart like Miss Shaw has to die.'

'That's understandable, Sophia, but make sure you keep that thought to yourself. He knows you're coming back and I'm dreading how he will react. In that way, nothing has changed.'

'What about Mother? Is she still the same?'

'Yes, unfortunately. She ignores everything that goes on; as long as she gets her fix she's fine. Manon's become their little drug mule - they barely leave the house now, apart from if they go to meet their friends. I don't think it'll be long until our sister starts dabbling herself; she's on track to become just like them.'

'The apple definitely didn't fall far from the tree with that one,' I nod. 'I know she's our sister but I'll never forget the time she found out my hiding place and told our father knowing he would beat me. From that moment, I've never looked at her as my sister.'

'Oh Sophia, don't say that!' Mireille compassionately says. 'Manon is just as much a victim as we are. She is a product of her upbringing too. She doesn't have the same strength as us and she's just doing what she can to get our parents' approval. It's a matter of survival. They use her and she lets them. I feel sorry for her as she'll end up just like them - but alone. We have each other but she has no one.'

As Mireille's words sink in, I pay attention to all families who pass us by as we make our way from the train station towards my childhood home; they seem so happy and normal, displaying a natural warmth and affection that is alien to me. A wave of sadness washes over me. What did we ever do to deserve being born to such cold, dysfunctional parents? I watch the cheery faces of the children as they walk hand-in-hand with their mothers and fathers, and I begin to wonder if I should have just left all this behind me for good? Cut all contact with my family and move on alone? But as I look at Mireille, my heart softens and I know I owe it to her to at least try. It isn't just about me anymore, I need to help Mireille escape this life too.

Seeing me struggle with my case, Mireille takes my it from me and wheels it behind her as she says: 'So, does this place ring any bells with you?'

'Yes, it's the palace park.' I am so happy to be here again. 'Never have I seen a prettier place. You took me to the palace gates when I was younger to try and catch a glimpse of Isabella, so I could see a real-life Princess.'

I close my eyes for a moment, inhaling the sweet aroma of the flowers in bloom. It's like a time warp - the gardeners carefully tending to the floral displays could be the same ones I saw as a child. Birds swarm happily around the fountain, which provides an oasis of refreshment as well as the most luxurious bird bath. Behind the park, perched upon the hill, lies the palace, visible but unreachable at the same time. How I'd love to live there, safe and secure. My father would never be able to touch me there . . .

'I used to love bringing you here because you'd always have the biggest smile on your face. See, just like that.' Mireille beams at me. 'It's the only time you ever got excited - it was the cutest thing to watch. You never smiled at home. Each time we came, despite never seeing Princess Isabella, you had such an unswerving hope that it would happen one day. Each and every time you were disappointed, but it never mattered, you were so pleased to just be here.'

'This was the happiest place of my whole childhood. Nothing bad happened here. It was just us. We were free of the fear that tainted every other second of our lives. Each time I came here, it was a respite from home and I loved it.'

'So . . . do you want to go up to the gates today and take a quick look, just like old times?'

'Let's leave it till another day,' I say after some thought. 'It'll be something for us both to look forward to.'

'That sounds a great idea. I'm so glad to have my little sister back, and to have the chance to get to know the person you've become.' Mireille links her free arm through mine and we leave the park, heading back to the place I once called home.

Despite only being a mile or so from the palace, our home couldn't be more different. As we approach the apartment block, it's clear that nothing much has changed. The building seems a little more dilapidated and the children's play equipment is rustier than when I left. As we ascend the needle-strewn staircase, the stench of urine fermenting in the humidity causes me to gag. I try to carry on but as I feel the vomit rising in my throat, I'm forced to leave and seek some fresh air.

'Sorry, Sophia, I should've warned you about the smell but I've just got used to it. Believe it or not, this isn't that bad. On a really hot day in the middle of summer even I struggle - so you'd have no hope.'

It's a shock after the clean and beautiful school I've been living in. 'I really hope you're joking,' I tell her. 'I can't imagine anything being worse than this.'

Mireille chuckles as she ushers me back into the stairwell to continue our ascent to the flat. Walking through the door, I'm surprised by how tidy it is. The only time I ever remember our place being tidy was when the social worker came to visit; other than that, it was always in a state.

'Sophia, is that really you? How sophisticated you look in your fancy clothes.' My mother grabs my hands in her own before embracing me. Her affection breeds suspicion; as a child I don't remember a time when she ever picked me up or cuddled me. While she rarely hit me directly, she always turned a blind eye when my father did. I always thought that she felt nothing for me - so this display must be more from curiosity than affection. After all, she hasn't seen me in eleven years, never once has she even tried to contact me.

'Thank you, Mother, that's very kind.' I break away and see Manon standing behind her. We never had much time for each other growing up but Mireille has made a good point that we are all in this together. In a lot of ways, I'm the lucky one to have gotten away when I did.

'Hello, Manon, it's good to see you again.'

'You too, Sophia. Welcome home.'

I hold the gaze of my mother and sister for a moment longer, absorbing the changes since I last saw them before taking a seat at the kitchen table. My mother's once brown hair is now grey, her face filled with lines from years of alcohol and drug abuse. As for Manon, I feel a pang of pity: she seems surrounded by a veil of sadness, her eyes hollow and her pretty face looks almost grey, her hair hangs straggly and unwashed around her shoulders. I don't know if I would have even recognised her, the difference in her is shocking.

Awkwardness hangs in the air; it's clear no one knows what to say. In truth, I'm a stranger within my own family, the only exception being Mireille because of the close connection we built up all those years ago.

The atmosphere eases when my mother and Manon leave the kitchen. Mireille joins me at the table with a bunch of magazines which she places in front of me.

'I've got something to show you, Sophia. I think you're going to like it.'

I watch as she flicks through the pages, gently biting on the corner of her lip as she gets closer to the page she wants to show me.

'Take a look at this picture - what do you see?'

I look down at a picture of Isabella at her birthday party, held on the same day as mine. Her chocolate-brown hair is artfully arranged into a chignon with curls falling around her face.

'She has really brown eyes, they're so pretty.' I look up at my sister to see an amused smile cross her face.

'Yes, that's true - but it's not what I meant. Are you sure you don't see anything else?'

I look again closely at the picture before turning to the next page where there is a full-length photograph of her ball gown. The scarlet-red satin dazzles the eye: it is corseted to the waist with a smattering of Swarovski crystals that glitter like stars in the midnight sky.

'Oh, it's the dress, it's just beautiful!'

'No, Sophia, doesn't she remind you of someone?' Mireille turns back to the original picture she showed me.

'No. I'm not following what you mean.'

'Well, I think she looks a lot like you in this photo. Do you really not see the resemblance?'

'Are you serious?' I scoff. 'Isabella's far more elegant and beautiful than I could ever be.'

'To me, she's your absolute double in this photo. Besides, if you were stood here in the same dress, as done up as she is, then you'd look elegant and beautiful too.'

'Aw, you're just saying that because I'm your sister, but thank you, Mireille. It's a lovely compliment. I wish I could have made a dress as fabulous as that though,' I say wistfully.

'Do you want to be a designer, Sophia? I could see you doing something like that. You always were very creative - if you were able to get your head out of a book long enough, that is.'

'Well, I've been making my own clothes for years. I really took to the sewing classes at school so I practised hard to develop my skills and now I'm quite good. This outfit is one I designed and made myself.' I point to my turquoise blue maxi dress, which I've teemed with the red accessories Miss Shaw bought for me before she died. 'It's one of my favourites actually.'

'Oh wow, I really thought that was a great outfit when I saw it but never dreamed you had made it yourself. Just look at my baby sister now, a fashion designer and a great one at that. I'm so proud of you.'

'Well, what's mine is yours, Mireille. Do you fancy a makeover?'

I see a smile cross her face as we go into the bedroom we always shared and I start to rummage through the clothes in my suitcase to see what will suit her. I pull out a dress and start to pin it up to make it smaller so that it will fit her petite frame perfectly.

The sudden slam of the front door signals my father's

return; instantly the hairs rise up on my arms, the old fear enveloping me just like it always did. Although I am now an adult, at this moment I still feel very much like the child I was when I left this flat. Sitting down on the edge of the bed, I wait, my heart thudding against my chest.

'*Mireille, get here now!*' our father roars, his words slurred as he stumbles down the hall. It's obvious that he's been to the pub, clearly nothing has ever changed.

'I'm coming, Father.' She motions at me to stay in the bedroom then rushes out of the door, closing it behind her to try and prevent my father barging in.

'What the hell are you wearing? And what's that muck on your face? Where did you get all this from? Miss Moneybags now, are we?'

'These are Sophia's clothes, and she let me borrow her make-up. You know I don't have any of my own.'

'I should have known *she* wouldn't be in this place five minutes without turning everything upside down,' he snarls. 'Where is the troublemaking little bitch?'

'She's asleep. It's been a long day for her and it's getting late so let's just leave her until tomorrow.'

There is a long silence before my father responds, his voice hardens.

'Leave her? Never! Now, get her up and bring her out here to greet me with the respect I deserve. Without me, she'd have nothing.'

I emerge from the room, ensuring I hold my head high and respond calmly.

'I'm here, Father, what do you want?' I look into his eyes, knowing that mine cannot hide the hatred I feel for him.

'Well, well, well . . . look what we have here,' he sneers. 'Haven't you grown up into a right snooty-nosed cow with her head firmly stuck up her own backside? You have become just like *her*, just like that devil of a woman I had the misfortune to call my Mother. She would have loved you, which is why I always have - and always will - despise you!'

He growls 'Now, who do you think you are, coming into my home, acting as if you own the place? I'm the head of the family, not you.'

Hoping to avoid an argument, I remain silent and lower my gaze to the ground.

'Don't you dare ignore me!' he thunders. 'Speak to me when I'm talking to you! I said *who - do - you - think - you - are*?'

I square my shoulders. 'Well, if you insist, Father, I think I'm the daughter of a weak man, so unable to cope with his life that he has to take his frustrations out on his defenceless daughters just to feel like a man. You, head of the household? Don't make me laugh! All you ever did was take the money meant to feed and clothe your children and spend it on drugs and alcohol. You aren't the head of anything. You're pathetic and I despise you too, seems that's another thing I have in common with my grandmother.'

He reaches out and grabs my chin, squeezing hard, as he pulls my face towards him.

'Don't you dare come in here and speak to me like that. I treated you the way you deserved to be treated. It's so easy, Sophia, to put the blame on me, but deep down you know you deserved everything you got. I'm sure it rots away at you at night, knowing that you couldn't even gain the love of your own father. What a failure you must be - and I look forward to watching you live a lonely, miserable life because we both know you are expecting so much more.

But you won't get it - I'll make sure of that.'

Anger bubbles up inside me as he releases my face and turns away with a smirk, the arrogant look of victory.

'Now that's where you're wrong because the only person disgracing themselves is you,' I say in a passionate but quivering voice. As I speak, years of hatred rise up and pour out of me. 'The resentment may burn in you over never gaining your mother's love but trust me, Father, I've never cared what you feel towards me. I *am* loved and that's what really burns, isn't it? Let me ask you this: do you tell your so-called friends about the way you hit and burnt your five-year-old child for kicks? You may make my life miserable while you are alive, Father, but rest assured that *I will dance on your grave when you die*.'

I have pushed him too far. The flame of maddened rage flickers behind his eyes - the same old danger sign - he launches himself at me, grabbing hold of my hair, dragging me across the floor.

Mireille tries to stop him but she's pushed violently into the table.

As the blows rain down on my torso, I'm a child again laying on the floor, cowering beneath my father. Suddenly, I realise I am no longer defenceless and I begin to fight back. The look of surprise on his face is followed by a lunge at me; as he tries to grip my neck in his hands. Instinctively, I raise my knees in defence, hitting him hard in the nose. He recoils in horror as the blood pours down his top.

For the first time, I see a look of fear in his eyes. I hold his stare, no longer intimidated or controlled by this excuse of a man.

'I'm treating you exactly as *you* deserve, Father. You taught me well.' The words fly like poisoned arrows out of my mouth, tipped with defiance and hatred.

'Get her out, get her out of my house!' he screams. 'Make sure that she never comes back - *ever*.'

Before another move can be made, I race past my father and sister, straight out of the door, and fly down the grotty stairwell into the night. The cool evening air hits me but still I keep running as if my life depends on it. I run on through the night, not even sure where I'm going, just following the streetlights in the hope that I'll find somewhere safe to stop. I've no money, no phone and nowhere to turn. There is no one who can help me.

As the streetlights end, I'm surrounded by darkness. Who knows what lurks within the shadows? I don't even know where I am. However, once my eyes adjust, the familiar outline of the palace gardens becomes visible. What a miracle, to have ended up in the only place in this city where I've ever felt safe!

Again, I start to run, pushing harder as I ascend the hill to the palace gates, unable to stop the tears spilling down my cheeks. The wrought-iron gates feel cold against my skin, and from sheer exhaustion I slump to the ground, unable to stand a minute longer.

Never before in my life have I felt so alone and so afraid.

Chapter 4

Bound by invisible chains with every step I take. My title is like a noose, tightening around me each day. Adulthood should have brought me freedom, but the expectation now is that I begin to take on my own royal duties.

Smiling to the waiting crowd now, I wave dutifully; inside, however, I wish I could be anywhere but here. Why can't I just be normal?

A sea of strange faces gaze at me with adoration, greeting me with gifts as if I'm a long-lost friend when they've never actually met me. How disappointed they would be to know how much I'd give to swap places with them, how I long to be just a face in the crowd. Why should I be put upon a pedestal just because I happen to have been born into royalty? Never will I understand how the shackles that bind me seem so attractive to those who have freedom, the only thing I've ever wanted.

As I go to make my very first public address, my nerves begin to rattle. When I open my mouth, will anything actually come out? Taking a deep breath, I say a little prayer before I begin.

'I would like to thank you all for coming out to support me today in my first solo engagement. As your future

Queen, I've a lot to learn and that learning starts today. To know that I have your support means a great deal to me. My greatest wish is that one day I will become a Queen that you can be proud of. That commitment doesn't begin sometime in the future but today, right now while I stand in front of you as your Princess. It is my belief that to become a Queen you can be proud of, I first have to become a Princess you can be proud of. I make that commitment to you today.'

The crowd cheers as I finish my speech. Staying in place for a moment longer, I feel a sense of relief that it's over. I give one final wave before climbing back into the limousine to return to the palace. Tears sting my eyes as I realise I've just given up my entire life for my father's dream. It's my destiny to be Queen - but should I not get the chance to experience life first - to know how it feels to live a life free from protocol and constraint? Should I have to pay such a high price for duty?

I know I need to accept that this is my life but I can't. Although I can guess my parents' reaction, I've never actually had the discussion with them. As the car pulls into the palace, I wonder if it would be worth trying. At least then I'd know.

Settling down at the table with my family for dinner, I can hardly eat a thing, trying to gauge the best time to broach this difficult subject. My chance comes at the end of the evening, while we're having coffee in the Blue Drawing Room.

'Isabella, my darling, we were so proud of you today,' my father says, my sisters raise their eyebrows at this. 'You're a natural when it comes to people, a born leader - and what a fine Queen you'll make.'

'Daddy, you know I don't like you saying that. I don't want to even consider a time without you or Mama.'

My mother gets up from her place and comes to sit beside me, putting an arm around me.

'You know, my love, that's exactly how I felt about my papa. I lost my mother at a young age and he was all I had; there wasn't anything I wouldn't do for him. I still miss him every day.'

'Your mother's devotion to her father knew no bounds,' my father agrees. Then he murmurs: 'There has always been three of us in this marriage.'

'Henri, how can you say such a thing – and in front of the children? That's not true at all. You both meant the absolute world to me!'

'I'm only teasing you, Charlotte. I always admired you for your devotion and it was one of the things that set you apart from anyone else.'

'Why did you never tell me that before? After all these years of marriage and you're still surprising me? It was your kindness that set you apart to me.'

She turns to us. 'Now, girls, you may not believe it but I wasn't short of admirers at your age. But each and every one of them was the same - pig-headed and acting as if I should be grateful for their attention while simultaneously never giving too much back. I was very like you, Isabella, fiercely independent and wanting someone who cared enough to be able to treat me as an equal, not a commodity.'

We huddle around her, fascinated, she goes on: 'I first met your father at a ball here. I had come with my friend, since her father worked at the palace. We all knew the Prince would be present; he was the most eligible man in the country but I honestly didn't care. The way I saw it, if

I couldn't find a normal guy who didn't have an ego as big as his head then there was not much hope for a Prince. But your father asked me to dance – he won me over and the rest is history, as they say.' She smiles at him. 'It really was quite the fairy-tale romance.'

I seize my cue, as I say, 'Mama, you are so right. Like you, I too am fiercely independent. Look, I want to be honest with you and Daddy. The truth is, I'm not happy. I want to have the chance to go to Paris, to be given time to live anonymously, just a normal teenager without the burden of my royal status. Kind of like a gap year I suppose but I only want a few months and I'd be staying in the same country. Please, can you let me go to Paris?'

My parents and siblings turn to look at each other in utter shock. The baffled expression on my father's face then turns to anger.

'What the hell has gotten into you, Isabella? How could you be so ungrateful! You're next in line to the throne and quite frankly it's insulting to hear you speak such nonsense. Your face has graced every magazine and television outlet in the world since the day you were born, so answer me this: *how can you be anonymous: how can you ever be normal*?'

I lower my head as my hopes and dreams desert me. Daddy's reaction is not wholly unexpected but it is disappointing. Is a little understanding too much to expect?

'I never asked to be a Princess,' I say choking back my tears. 'How was I to know that in order to wear the crown I had to throw my whole life away. Did you ever ask me if that was OK? Did you ever ask me what I wanted? All I'm asking for is the chance to find out what it's like to live beyond the prison gates of this place.'

'Insolent girl! I can't talk to you right now or I'll lose my temper completely.' Fury dances across my father's face, his jaw hardening as he turns away to leave the room, slamming the door behind him. My tears fall as I realise that my whole life will be dictated by duty and protocol. That I'll never be free.

Giving my sisters permission to go to their rooms, my mother passes me a tissue and allows me to pull myself together before walking me back to my room.

'*Love,* I do understand how you feel. I've long seen that you inherited that restless part of my nature, the part that seeks adventure and excitement. But your father's right, you can't be the ordinary person that you want to be - not because of the title we placed upon you at birth - but because of the public's expectation of you. You're not a Princess just in title, Isabella, you're a Princess in the hearts and minds of a nation. That's what makes you so special, and that's why you can never know what it's like to be normal.'

I see that there are tears in her own eyes; that she too has sacrificed her freedom for her marriage to the King.

'Oh Mama, I don't mean to sound ungrateful but these walls feel like a jail. I can't leave without permission, I can't do *anything* without permission!'

'The world is a cruel place at times, love. What you don't realise is that for every person who stands in adoration of you as a member of the royal family, there are many others who would wish to hurt you for exactly the same reason. We spend a fortune on security because it's necessary. You're not a prisoner, Isabella, but you can't just wander out on your own because the danger is too great.'

'If I'm honest, Mama, the way I feel right now, I'd take the chance.'

'Oh Isabella, you're far too much like me for your own good,' she says, looking at me sympathetically. She promises: 'I'll have a word with your father, maybe see if we can arrange a trip to Paris for you. I'm sure we could tie it in with some engagements. It's the best we can do, my love.'

'Thank you, Mama.' I yawn and cover my mouth. 'It's getting late. I think I'll just go to bed if you don't mind.'

My mother nods then kisses me good night before leaving my room, I feel the weight of her gaze upon me before she closes the door behind her.

Lying on my bed, I replay the evening's events. A sudden thought crosses my mind. Racing to the window, I look down at the ground outside my bedroom. It's not too far. Then, before I can change my mind, I whip off my sheet and duvet cover, knotting them together, along with a big towel from my bathroom, attaching my homemade rope to a bar on my window. Tucking my credit card into my jeans pocket, I stand on a chair, climb out backwards and carefully descend to the ground, clinging to the rope, my heart pounds a million beats to the second. Once on the ground, my knees shake slightly as I set off out into the night.

The cool summer air surrounds me as I hurry towards the palace gates before someone can stop me. I've no idea what I'll do when I'm on the other side of the gates but I don't care. I want my freedom and I won't take no for an answer. I'm an adult, aren't I? Surely, I get to make my own decisions now.

Just as I reach the gates, however, I see an unexpected

sight: a slumped figure lies sobbing in front of them. I approach gingerly.

'Are you OK?' I ask.

The figure quickly rises, wiping away the tears before turning around to face me. I see that it's a frightened-looking girl, around the same age as me.

'No, not really. I'm sorry, I had nowhere else to go and this felt like the safest place to come.'

The girl seems sincere. 'Don't apologise,' I say, not wanting to see her cry. 'Why do you have nowhere left to go? Can't you go home?'

'Home? No, my father kicked me out.' She pulls up her sleeve, and even in the shadows, I can make out the angry bruises covering her arms.

'That's dreadful - you poor thing. Wait there one moment and I'll get someone to open the gates.'

I rush off to get help, feeling a buzz of excitement as to who this stranger could be. I return with a guard who dutifully opens the gate to let her in.

'Thank you, Michel,' I tell him. 'You may leave us now.'

'As you wish, Your Royal Highness.' The guard walks off as instructed.

'Isabella? Are you Princess Isabella?' the girl asks, her eyes wide.

'Yes, that's right. Now, I've a slight confession. You see, I climbed out of my bedroom window so we'll need to get back in that way. Are you good at climbing?'

Immediately she responds with: 'Well, I'm always up for a challenge, let's put it that way, Your Highness.'

I smile at the stranger's response.

We manage to haul ourselves back up into the bedroom before I pull up the homemade rope and unknot it all again. It's hard, since the knots have grown tight from the strain of our weight.

'Here, let me do that for you,' the girl offers, I notice she doesn't use my royal title this time, which I like. She deftly untangles the items and proceeds to put the sheet and duvet cover back on my bed.

'Sorry, forgive my manners,' I say. 'I haven't asked your name.'

'My name is Sophia - Sophia Lazarus.'

'Sophia's a pretty name, it suits you. Please take a seat. Now Sophia Lazarus, let me see your arms again.'

She slowly rolls up her sleeves, turning her head away as I look down at the angry marks covering her arms.

'I'm so sorry for you, this is just shocking. You don't deserve to be treated like that - and by your own father! It's appalling. Although ironically, the reason I was outside at this hour is because I had a big argument with my father tonight too, so maybe there's something in the air. He would never hurt me though; his bark is worse than his bite.'

Sophia politely perches on the end of my bed before surveying my room in wonder. The more I observe her, the more I see that we look quite alike. Her hair is the same chocolate-brown as mine, as are her dark eyes and eyelashes, even the slightly olive hue to her skin . . . It's bizarre!

Surprisingly, she says: 'Isabella, you won't believe it when I tell you this but we were born on the same day, only two hours apart. What a small world, eh?'

'That's an insane coincidence,' I agree, 'especially considering we actually look quite alike. In fact, the more I'm looking at you the more I'm convinced of it.'

'It's funny you should say that - my sister Mireille said the same thing just today. She thinks in one of the pictures from your birthday that you're my double.'

I feel a surge of hope rise in me as I decide to put my theory to the test.

'Take down your hair and give it a brush so it's the same as mine,' I suggest. 'I think we need to switch clothes - that'll be the real test as to how much we look alike.'

We put on each other's outfits and as I look at Sophia stood in my cream jeans and pale blue sleeveless blouse, it's like looking in the mirror.

'We could be twins,' I gasp. 'This is amazing! Even my own sisters don't look as much like me as you do.'

Sophia frowns. 'Now you're in my clothes, the resemblance really is uncanny.'

Stood in Sophia's turquoise blue maxi dress and red accessories, her outfit is really stylish and it fits me so well that I wish it were mine.

'Did you say you didn't have anywhere to go?' I ask her.

'That's right.' The other girl looks rueful. 'I ran out of the house without my phone or any money after my father attacked me, so until tomorrow I've nowhere to turn. Luckily though it's only one night then I can get my things and call my friend for help.'

'If you're interested,' I say carefully, 'I have a proposition for you.' I take a deep breath. 'You see, more than anything in the world, I want my freedom. I want to walk down the street without anyone knowing who I am. To just be normal. That's what I was arguing about with my father tonight because he doesn't understand. He wants me to just follow in his footsteps, for him to teach me how to be a great Queen, but I just can't carry on never knowing what it's like outside these walls.' I summon my courage. 'So, if I suggested to you that we switch places for a week, would you do it?'

There is a moment of astonished silence before my new friend manages to speak.

'Oh, Isabella,' she stutters, 'I'd love that more than anything! It would literally be a dream come true for me too - but are you sure we could pull it off without getting caught?'

'Oh yes, I've no doubt about that. Here's how. I'll take my credit card so I'll have money to travel to Paris and pay for my accommodation. In one week's time I'll return at midnight, when you'll come to the palace gates and order the guard to let me in, just like I did tonight. At which point we switch back again. It's totally fool-proof. My parents will be very busy next week and I have no engagements, so it should work easily.'

I see Sophia mulling over the idea in her head, the concentration evident on her face.

Finally, she responds: 'OK, Isabella, you're on.' I see her beam with excitement. 'What do I need to know?'

'Thank you so much, Sophia, you're an absolute angel. If I didn't know better I'd think it was fate.'

As I begin to fill Sophia in on the finer details of life as a Princess, there's an unexpected knock at my door. 'Come in,' I call out, giving Sophia a warning glance - and to my dismay, my mother and father walk in.

'Isabella, I wanted to talk to you. . .' My father's words trail off when he sees that I'm not alone.

'Who are you and what are you doing in my daughter's bedroom?' he demands. To my surprise, the distinctly hostile question is directed at me. Of course - I'm still in

Sophia's clothes. I turn to Sophia, silently signalling to her that I want her to go along with it.

'Well, Father, I can explain. You see, this is my friend Sophia and we were just talking.' I hear the hesitation in her voice but continue to smile in support. My heart beats faster than it ever has as a rush of excitement fills me.

'Isabella, when did you start calling me Father?' the King demands, looking even more dissatisfied. I quickly mouth the word *Daddy* to Sophia.

'Sorry, Daddy, you've just caught me off-guard.'

'I know when you're lying, Isabella, but if you want to believe that I'm stupid, then fine. Your friend here has to leave - and she has to leave *now*.'

'Very well, Daddy, I'll see her out. Please come this way, Sophia.' She turns to look at me and I smile back at her, scarcely able to comprehend that I'll be able to just walk out of the door. If we can fool my parents, then we can fool everyone.

As my parents follow us to the door, at each step of the way I'm convinced we'll be uncovered - but they eventually turn towards their quarters and we continue to the palace gates alone.

'I'm sorry that you'll have to deal with my father,' I tell Sophia. 'He has a temper on him but he's really very kind. If you say that you're sorry, that you've thought about what he said, that you understand your position, it'll all iron itself out. Thank you so much again, Sophia. Now if you go up to that hut and command the guard to let me out, I'll be gone.'

'Are you sure you'll be all right?' she asks. 'Do you have everything you need?'

'Oh, wait no - my credit card, it's in your jeans pocket.

Thank God you reminded me.'

Sophia reaches into the pocket of the jeans and hands me my credit card, saying, 'Have a fantastic time, Isabella, enjoy every minute of it and I'll see you in a week.'

Before I leave, I give Sophia one last hug - after which I walk into the night, leaving behind the title that has shackled me all these years. The moon illuminates my path, guiding me with her silver light as I make my way towards the life everyone said I couldn't have.

Chapter 5

Standing alone in the stillness of the night, I watch Isabella walk away to freedom. She stops briefly, turning back to wave goodbye. Clearly, she feels no fear, just joy at escaping her royal shackles. However, my own misgivings refuse to subside. Are we making a big mistake? Does she even know how to look after herself? It all feels so irresponsible. But I hold onto the fact that I'm helping her achieve an impossible dream - and it isn't as if money will ever be an issue for her; she'll never be in need of anything.

Inhaling deeply, I seek to find my way back to her room, hoping that we're as alike in courage and daring as we are in looks.

Following the exact same path back to the palace, I've barely entered before the King and Queen stop me in my tracks.

Quickly averting my eyes from their penetrating gaze, beads of sweat start to form on my forehead. I know I can't avoid the two of them for ever, but tonight I need to try because I'm in no position to be convincing yet. I'm still in a state of shock after everything and I need time to process what has happened before the questions start.

Just as I feared, the questions begin immediately.

'Do you want to explain to us what's going on?' the King demands. 'We're both worried about your behaviour, it's so out of character.'

'I've said everything I need to, Fath— sorry, I mean Daddy. It's been a long day and I just want to go to bed now if you don't mind.'

But the King's face hardens- my hands start to shake as he begins to remind me of my father.

'I do mind, Isabella,' he snaps. 'How do you think we feel when we come to your rooms to find a stranger there? How do you even know her?'

'Sophia Lazarus is a friend of a friend, and she's a very nice person, Daddy,' I manage to say. 'Look, I'm sorry for what I said earlier. I do understand my position and I know you're only looking out for me. If I'm honest, I feel a little unwell this evening so I just want to go to bed.'

I see the King and Queen look at each other before the Queen walks over and links arms with me before walking me back to Isabella's suite. Secretly, I'm relieved as I'm not sure I'd have found my way back there.

'Goodnight, love. You get some rest and we can talk about it in the morning.'

'Mother, I'd really like to just drop the subject completely if that's OK? Let's just start afresh tomorrow, shall we?'

The Queen looks almost hurt before quickly regaining her composure and giving me a small smile before leaving to re-join the King.

As the door shuts, I feel an enormous sense of relief. Finally, I'm able to be alone and have some time to think about what is actually happening.

In awe of how beautiful this room is, I notice three doors opening off it. Walking through the first one I come to a sitting room, a large semi-circular room with wall-to-ceiling bay windows to the front with little seats in them. A large and fluffy corner sofa is placed to one side, opposite a massive flat-screen TV. Two elegant chairs sit proudly in front of the windows with a bookshelf tucked away in the corner. I pick up a book to take with me before I leave the room. Just like me, the Princess is a fan of dystopian fiction, selecting 'The Hunger Games' I make my way back to the main room.

Putting the paperback down on the bed, I walk through the other door to find a bathroom, with the centrepiece being a large jacuzzi bath. Fresh clean towels are neatly stacked into a little tower on a cabinet to the side of the bath. Excitedly, I turn the taps on, adding some bubble bath that fills the room with its sweet aroma.

Leaving the bath to run, I simply have to find out what's behind the third door. Swinging it open, I realise that I've found Isabella's dressing room. In the corner is an ornate dressing-table; perfumes and make-up are arranged in tidy rows. A matching chest of drawers is where I find a pair of Isabella's pyjamas. A small wardrobe is next to the chest of drawers – but surely Isabella has more clothes than would fit into that? Keen-eyed, I gaze around the room. A trio of full-length mirrors hang opposite a raised platform in the middle of the room. This must be where she puts on her evening dresses, I assume.

I spot another door at the rear of the room and as I walk through, the mystery is solved. This is her walk-in wardrobe, and every wall is lined with racks and cupboards full of the most amazing clothes and accessories. How is it possible that one person can own so many outfits? I notice how alike our tastes seem to be and find myself slightly amused at this, given the massive discrepancy in our backgrounds. I take keen notice of the designers' names, thinking that perhaps, one day Isabella might be wearing a Lazarus original design . . .

I suddenly remember that the bath is still running! Racing back to the bathroom, I just manage to catch it before the water overflows, I let some out to ensure it doesn't slop over the side when I get in. Carefully removing Isabella's jeans and top, I stand in my own plain underwear, catching a glimpse of my bruises in the mirror, scattered across my arms and torso, pain radiating from them with every move I make. The warmth of the bath feels soothing and the discomfort melts away.

What a peculiar day, how could I have known when I ran away from my father that I would end up swapping places with a Princess. It sounds ridiculous! Lying back in the scented water, I wonder how Isabella is getting on. I feel worried for her, praying that she's safely tucked up in a hotel somewhere and not wandering the streets of the city alone, like I was, only hours earlier. I hope that the sheltered life she's lived doesn't mean that she sees no evil in this world.

Getting out of the bath and into the nice clean pyjamas, I climb into bed and rest my head on the pillow. I open the book but begin to doze, realising that while I'm here, I'm truly safe. There is no way my Father can ever reach me here - and for that I'm eternally grateful. While Isabella looked at these gates as a prison, to me they are a fortress representing protection, a world away from the life I was sent back to. The life I hated, even as a child . . .

'Wakey wakey, sleepyhead!'

I open my eyes to see a strange woman in my room. She's around the same age as the Queen, and has short hair, cut into a pixie bob, and a very petite frame. As she opens the curtains, I pull the covers up to my face.

'Is everything alright?' she asks curiously. 'You're looking at me as if I'm a complete stranger. Have you forgotten me during the night, Isabella?'

'Of course not, it's just I'm still half-asleep.'

'We heard that you had a strange girl in here last night. Now, I could have sworn it would be the boys you were smuggling into your room but I'm not here to judge.' The woman winks at me. 'I'm very open-minded.'

'It was a friend of mine, that's all. I can't believe Mother and Father have been telling everyone.'

The woman stops what she is doing and stares at me - I feel the weight of her gaze upon my face as if she's trying to find something in my features to give away who I really am. I feel my cheeks begin to flush from her scrutiny.

'Isabella, since when have you called your parents "Mother" and "Father"?'

'Ah, Celeste, there you are. When you're done with Isabella can you please go and find Baptiste - he's asking after you.'

I look up as two young girls walk into my room. The one who spoke has blonde hair, and the other has dark hair like Isabella's.

'Of course, Alix. I'll just finish up here then I'll go to find him.'

'Isabella, what are you doing in bed at this time?' asks the other one. 'It's very unlike you.'

'I'm feeling a little under the weather.'

'That's an understatement,' I hear Celeste mutter under her breath.

'Come on, you need to get dressed. Mama and Daddy are expecting us for breakfast. You've never kept us waiting before, Isabella. This is all very strange.' Alix and the other girl look at me suspiciously.

'So, they're my sisters,' I murmur to myself - but immediately realise that I have said it too loudly.

Celeste gapes at my sisters in horror before they all turn to stare at me. I break eye contact, not having a clue what to do.

'Yes, that's right, we're your little sisters, Isabella. I'm Alix and I'm 16 and this is Grace and she's 13. Are you sure you're OK? You haven't been taking drugs, have you?'

I notice that Alix looks much more like the King while Grace and Isabella take after the Queen with their dark hair and eyes.

'Of course not!' I say firmly. 'It's just been a difficult few days,' which is the truth, 'and I just need a little extra rest. It's nothing to worry about.' A nervous yawn escapes me.

Alix moves towards me and rests the back of her hand upon my forehead, which is damp and clammy from the stress.

'You're certainly feeling a little hot. Do you want me to tell Mama and Daddy that you're not well enough to come down for breakfast? We can send you something up instead.'

'Yes, I think that would be the best idea. I really need to rest for a bit.' It's such a relief, to be given the opportunity to put off meeting the King and Queen again for a little while longer.

'I can't deny that I'm worried about you,' Alix goes on.

'We all are because you seem so out of sorts. I just want you to know that you can talk to me if you need to. Please don't think that you have to go through this alone because you don't. At the end of the day, we're family and we need to stick together.'

'Thanks,' I say weakly. 'That means a lot to me but please don't worry. I'll be fine, honestly.'

'Well, if you need anything you know where to find us.'

I watch as everyone leaves the room, well aware that it's only a matter of time until I have to face them all. I've only delayed the inevitable. Despite supposedly having grown up in this palace, I don't have a clue where anything is. How am I possibly going to explain my sudden onset of amnesia?

As I lay my head back down on the pillow, I realise that what started as a dream is quickly turning into a nightmare.

Chapter 6

Striding out of the gates, I hasten my steps, the of fear hearing my name being called or the shuffle of feet running behind me causes my heart to pound in panic. I try to remain calm. When I'm a good distance away, and it's clear that no one has come after me, I take a moment to conceal myself in an alleyway and survey my surroundings. It feels amazing to be out here alone. Free! Finally, I will have the chance to meet people as myself, instead of being shackled to an archaic title that commands people to treat me differently.

The streetlight emits a soothing orange glow as I continue to head towards the city centre. The shops are still open for customers, but they will be closing in another hour or so, and then the streets will be deserted, not keen to be out alone at that point I carry on towards the hotel.

I know this first-ever taste of freedom may not last. Our daring plot could well be foiled, and I may have to return home to my parents and once again be imprisoned within the palace walls. But right now, I have my freedom - and I am determined to enjoy every single second of it! I see the Palais Royal Hotel come in to view. This stunning building was the home of my ancestors until 1875 when it was decommissioned as a royal residence and renovated into a beautiful hotel. So many times, I've been driven past it over the years, feeling sad that I would never be able to stay there. But that all changes tonight.

For a few moments, I stand and take in the beautiful aspect. The clock-tower rises majestically above the city, appearing to stretch all the way to the stars. The shimmering moonlight adds to the mystique of the gothic architecture of a bygone era. Then, not wishing to draw too much attention to myself, I enter the hotel.

'Good evening, Mademoiselle, how may I help you?'

Smiling back at the friendly face of the receptionist, I brace myself for a hint of recognition - but it doesn't come and clearly to her I'm just another paying customer. My confidence surges at this and I start to relax.

'Good evening,' I say politely, conscious that it must seem odd that I've arrived with no luggage. 'I'm sorry it's so late but I wondered if you had a room available for tonight?'

When the receptionist taps her computer, the clicking sound tells me she has manicured nails. Mama always loves her nails to be perfectly manicured; she's a firm believer that these tiny details should never be overlooked.

'We only have a double room available for tonight, which will be priced at €350 including a single person supplement and breakfast. Will that suit, Mademoiselle?'

I nod in agreement and wait while the receptionist finishes tapping into her computer.

'May I ask you to fill out these details for me, tick whether you would like to be added to our mailing list and to sign here and here, please.'

My heart sinks as I stare down at the form to see that it asks for my name and address. There's no way out of this: I'll have to put my actual name because that's the name on my bank card. In horror, I notice the form asks for a valid ID but my passport is locked away and with my parents. I pray she doesn't ask me. My nerves begin to flutter as I impulsively decide to use Eddie's address in Paris. I can't possibly put my real address, can I? I hand back the completed form along with my card, hoping that the woman isn't familiar with the official surname of my family and smile back at her trying to disguise the anxiety I'm feeling right now.

'Thank you, Mademoiselle Bourbon. I'll just put your card through for pre-authorisation. It's just to ensure that there are enough funds in your account and place a hold on the amount which we'll debit on your departure. Right - that's all done for you now. You're in Room 317 on the first floor. Do you have any luggage with you that you need us to bring up for you?'

The question I had been dreading. 'No, thank you,' I say in a dignified voice. I quickly make up a story about having a row with my boyfriend and walking out in my mind, just in case she enquires any further.

'The rooms are fully equipped with toiletries,' she tells me tactfully. 'You should find everything you need.'

'Thank you. Can you please ensure a hairbrush and some face cream are brought up to my room? Will you allow me to pay for this in the morning too?' She nods in agreement and smiles, I take the key card and walk towards the lifts, looking up at the impressive ceilings and the wrap-around balcony foyers on each floor. Chandeliers hang high above the marble floors, adding light and grandeur to the surroundings.

When I open the door to my room, I'm surprised by

just how lovely it is. The king-size bed is elegant and comfortable, and the décor perfectly sets off the antique bedroom furniture. The bathroom appears to be carved completely out of marble, including the luxury bath. Tucked in the corner is a massive shower that gleams as the light ricochets off the steel and glass.

I haven't been in the room long before a sudden knock at the door startles me – it's room service with my items. I thank the concierge with a pang of guilt that I have nothing to tip him with. Closing the door behind me, I put the items down on the bed and return to the bathroom.

There I find a toothbrush, toothpaste and mouthwash, as well as a luxury brand of soap, shampoo and shower gel. It feels so good to be able to have a quick shower and brush my teeth before heading to bed.

I feel completely exhausted – unsure if I'm in a state of shock or excitement about how things have turned out. Laying my head upon the pillow, I recall the strange turn of events. Confused by how this all actually happened. I feel so happy to finally be free, but I wish I could have prepared Sophia more. She has no way of knowing about the protocols or what it's like to be royal. I just hope she can find her way through all the challenges. I can't help but wonder how we'd get on, if we had met in different circumstances. Would we have been friends? I think we might have been as Sophia is by far the most interesting person I've ever met - and after this is all done and we've returned to our old lives, I hope we may be able to stay in touch.

The birds chirp noisily outside my window, waking me up

early. Ever since I can remember I've woken with the birds each morning. Quickly, I get myself showered and dressed, not wanting to waste any time. Since I'm used to having fresh clean clothes to wear each day, I decide the first thing I must do is buy some new outfits, a suitcase and some shoes. A shopping spree is definitely on the cards. Then comes the part I've been waiting for, to travel to Paris.

As I prepare to leave my room for breakfast, there's an unexpected knock at the door. I'm not expecting anyone. Opening the door, I see two police officers stood before me.

'Good morning, Mademoiselle. Are you Isabella Bourbon?'

My hearts sinks, I had hoped for a little more time. But it looks like the ruse has been unmasked, so there's nothing I can do but return home. Tears come to my eyes but I try hard to fight them back.

'Yes, that is correct.' I see the officers smirk at each other, their disrespectful behaviour is surprising.

'As in Her Royal Highness Princess Isabella of the House of Bourbon? Heir to the French throne?'

'Yes. As I said before, that is correct.' I'm beginning to lose patience with their attitude towards me. 'Look, I can explain everything. It isn't what you think.' The tears threaten to spill as I realise when they take me back to the Palace, how much I'll be losing.

One of the men snorts as he tries to stifle his laughter. 'Well, that's a new one on me. I mean, I've arrested two Jesuses, one Harry Potter and three Elvises before - but never a Princess.' The two police officers crack up at this, I wait impatiently for them to compose themselves.

'You're not going to arrest a Princess because I've done

nothing wrong,' I say, unable to hide my annoyance at them.

The older one loses his smile immediately and he tells me: 'You're right that we're not going to arrest a Princess - but we are going to arrest you, because you've committed fraud. You've used a credit card in the name of Princess Isabella which is a criminal act punishable by the law of the land. If you come with us, Mademoiselle, we'll take you down to the station.'

'You'll not be taking me anywhere,' I say haughtily. 'I *am* Isabella and it is my card. There has been no fraud as it is my own money. You will not touch my credit card because it belongs to me. You may apply to the palace and speak to the King if you don't believe me.'

I watch as the policemen try manfully to stifle their giggles once again and attempt to regain their authority.

'Oh, we're going to enjoy having you in custody, Mademoiselle. You really are quite the comedian. You should be on the TV.'

For heaven's sake! They really need to watch what they are saying.

'I *am* the eldest daughter of King Henri and my father would be very upset if he knew how you were talking to me. I don't think either of you are being professional at all. You're a disgrace!'

'We're very sorry, Your Highness,' the older one says with mock humility. 'Well, since we're in the company of royalty, we'll give you the VIP treatment and allow you to walk to the car without the handcuffs. See? We know how to treat a Princess, don't we, Sarge?'

'It's quite clear that you don't believe me, so please don't patronise me with your sarcasm.'

'Just answer me one thing, Mademoiselle,' says the sergeant, clearly confident he's going to prove me wrong. 'If you're really Princess Isabella, then who's the person in the palace? Pray, do enlighten us, Mademoiselle.'

'That's Sophia Lazarus,' I say tiredly. 'I met her at the palace gates last night. She had run away from home so I took her into the palace, and when I noticed how alike we looked, I asked her to switch places – just for one week. I took my credit card with me and came here. I'm off to Paris today.'

I see a frown cross the first police officer's face as we walk towards the patrol car. His anger evident as he turns on me and says, 'So, Princess Isabella is kind enough to take pity on you, paying you the greatest compliment by allowing you into her private domain - and you repay her by stealing her credit card? That's truly a despicable betrayal. It's clear to me that we're looking at theft as well as fraud.'

'Why won't you listen to me? Why won't you believe me that I am Isabella? I am the true Princess. Ask me any question - go on, ask me!'

The older one sighs, growing tired of my assertions. 'I think you've been reading far too many books. It's clear you're living in a fairy-tale but I'm afraid this is reality, not Disneyland. In the real world, theft and fraud are taken very seriously. Now get in the car, please. You're in a lot of trouble.'

'Fine, if you don't believe me then as I said before: ask my parents. They saw both of us in the room and they will know that I switched places because I've told them how much I wanted to be free from the palace. In fact, if you must know, we had a row about it. They will realise at once that I'm truly their daughter, and they will be so relieved to have me back again. If you get me to my parents then this will all be resolved.'

'I hate to break it to you, Your Highness, but we don't have a hotline to the King and Queen. We deal with their staff - so you won't be getting anywhere near them. Besides, there's no way we'd be informing them about your deluded claims to be their daughter. That would just be embarrassing and bring the police force into disrepute.'

Sudden tears spill down my cheeks as I realise that no one's ever going to believe me. After all, why would they? Even I have to admit that my story does sound far-fetched. What is going to happen now? Clearly, I'm not going to be returned home. Oh no! How will I be punished? I feel guilty that all this will be recorded in Sophia's name - when all she's done is try to help me.

Down at the station, the cell door is slammed shut behind me, I feel utterly desolate. To think that only a few hours ago I believed that the worst thing that could happen to me was being returned home once my identity had been uncovered.

How wrong could I be?

Having had my liberty taken away from me - for the second time - and not knowing how long this is going to last, I accept that I've gone from the frying pan into the fire - into a situation that is so much worse than the one I left behind. As I recall the conversation I had with Eddie, I feel like an idiot, but most of all I feel selfish. Did I really think about how this would affect Sophia? After all, this criminal conviction will affect her more than me, and as I sit here I wonder if I've just ruined her entire life with my own stupidity.

Chapter 7

Lying wide awake in the dead of night, I wait until the castle is sleeping before I set out to explore.

Tugging the bed covers aside, I creep towards the door and place my ear against it. There isn't even the smallest sound from outside, so I open it quietly and slip out of Isabella's room into the corridor. It's imperative that I learn where everything is if I stand any chance of making this venture work.

The silver glow of the moon gives an unearthly feel to the palace as I begin to descend the staircase. Standing in the centre of the foyer I gaze towards the corridors leading off it. Which one should I take first? Am I going to get lost?

'Ahem, Princess, isn't it a little late for you to be roaming round the palace?'

I jump with fright. Stood before me is a portly little man. His glasses sit strangely on his long nose. I try not to stare but he has an almost comical appearance, with his stern demeanour in perfect contrast to his comical look.

'I couldn't sleep, sir,' I manage to say. 'I just needed to stretch my legs.'

'Isabella, why do you call me sir? If your father heard you, I'd be in trouble. I'm here to serve you, not the other way around.'

I sigh deeply. It's difficult to be treated as if you are on a pedestal. I never thought I'd say it, but I miss being treated like me.

'If I told you a secret, would you promise to keep it?' I ask him. 'I need to tell someone or I'll go mad - but you must promise you'll never say anything.' I'm taking a big risk, but I don't see any alternative.

'I'm the soul of discretion, dear Princess, and I swear I won't reveal your secret to anyone. I tell you what, let's go and have a cup of chocolat chaud and you can tell me all about it.'

He's so comforting and kind. My spirits lift a little as I follow the man down to the kitchens, trying to discreetly make mental notes on how to get back. The man pulls out a chair for me at a table, quietly pottering around making the hot chocolate, bringing it to the table with some chocolate madeleines. He conveys an air of calm that helps me to relax slightly.

'I thought you might like a little treat, Princess, you need to keep your strength up, and I know these are your favourites.'

'Thank you, that's so sweet of you.' I am suddenly ravenous. I take a sip of the sweet chocolate drink and nibble on a delicious chocolate biscuit, all the while keeping my focus on the man and his kind face. Is it the right thing to do, to speak? Will he really keep my secret – or will I ruin everything?

'So, Isabella, what is it that's bothering you? I know your parents are very concerned, as you haven't been yourself these past few days. Come on now, you can tell old Baptiste what the trouble is.'

I swallow a piece of biscuit and say: 'Well, that's just it. You see, I'm not who you think I am. The reason I'm acting so oddly is because I'm not Isabella and I don't know anyone here. I've no idea who you are.'

A wary look crosses the man's face, his penetrative stare maps my face trying to find a trace of difference in my face. His brow knits together as he fails to do so.

'I can't believe that. I've known Isabella since she was a baby and looking at you now I see the same child I always have. But your explanation does account for your odd behaviour – unless you are ill, my poor child. Oh, I just don't know what to think! If it's true, how could this have happened?'

'Please don't tell anyone,' I beg urgently. 'It's a secret and it must stay that way. Promise me you won't say a thing and I'll tell you everything.'

'As long as you are not in danger, of course, I won't say a thing. To be honest, I don't think anyone would believe me anyway. I'm not sure I can believe it myself.'

'It happened the night that Isabella had the big argument with her father about going to Paris. She was really upset and decided to run away. We met at the palace gates, I had fled after my father attacked me, when Isabella found me crying at the gates she brought me to her room. When she saw how alike we looked, she suggested that we exchange places for a week.' I gulp. 'She was desperate for a taste of freedom and I was desperate for some security . . .'

I pull up my sleeves, showing him the bruises upon my arms.

'My name is Sophia Lazarus. My family live on the Forest estate– after fleeing my home I had nowhere else to go so I came to the palace because it's the only place I've ever felt safe.

The kindly man's face goes pale. 'Oh, my word. What a terrible thing to do to anyone, let alone your own child. I'm so sorry for you.'

'Isabella was ready to make her escape, but when she found me there, slumped and weeping in pain, she got the guard to let me in and we climbed back up a makeshift rope to her room.' I can't help but smile at the memory. 'It was one of the strangest nights of my life I still can't believe that it really happened.'

'I see. So *that's* how she came to have a stranger in her bedroom when the King and Queen walked in . . . Things certainly make a lot more sense now. And I can't deny this does sound exactly the kind of crazy thing that she would do. Good heavens, it's quite a shock.'

'It was clear how much it meant to Isabella to have her freedom and I needed somewhere to stay and so it seemed a good idea, although I wasn't sure when she first suggested it.'

The man nods understandingly, and I carry on.

'At first, I was worried we'd get caught but when we both had our hair styled the same way, and stood in each other's clothes, even I have to admit that we could have been twins. It was then that we agreed to switch for a week, after which she would return here to the gates at night, when we would swap back. But before she could tell me anything that could help, the King and Queen walked in. They instantly thought Isabella was me, we were still in each other's clothes, and the King told *her* to leave - so that's exactly what she did. She walked right out of the palace gates.'

I wait, scared of what will happen next as the man shakes

his head from side to side in disbelief.

'Oh Isabella, what have you done?' he groans. 'The folly of youth . . . Don't you know that nothing ever goes to plan in life?' He addresses me: 'How did she think you would be able to take her place when you know nothing about royal life? It was very unkind of her. No wonder everyone thinks that you've lost your mind.'

I recoil. 'Is that what they are all saying? How rude!'

'Come on - what are people supposed to think when you can't even recognise your own sisters or Celeste who has known you from the day you were born.' The man sighs heavily. 'I'm Baptiste, by the way, I'm the King's Equerry and the longest-serving member of staff. There isn't anything I don't know about palace life.'

I feel a stab of hope. 'Really? Can you help me learn what I need to know? Oh please, Baptiste, I don't want to let Isabella down! She so badly needed this chance to try out life on her own terms. She deserves that opportunity; would you want your daughter caged up like Isabella has been all her life?

He nods soberly. 'I understand. But this isn't a game. If anyone found out that I knew what was going on, I'd lose my job, which I love, and my reputation would be in tatters. I am betraying the King and Queen by colluding with you both. My dear, you need to understand exactly what it is you are asking of me. Have you ever thought that the best thing to do is to tell the truth and make sure that we get Isabella back where she belongs?'

'Baptiste, it's too late. We need to succeed in this because if it ever gets out, Isabella will be in real danger. Can you imagine the media frenzy? Would you really want her out there alone with everyone knowing who she really is?

You know I'm right. The only way we can keep her safe is if people really believe that *I am her*. I need your help, Baptiste, I can't do this without you. Besides, it's only for a few days and then everything will be back to normal, I promise. No one will ever know.' Inwardly I pray that this is true, that things do go to plan.

He sits for a time and ponders, before making up his mind.

'I clearly have no choice,' he says finally. 'These walls have ears sometimes and you never know what will end up in the papers. I couldn't guarantee it wouldn't get leaked so I agree, we need to make this work. You are right, Sophia, it *is* the only way to keep the Princess safe - not to mention the scandal that would ensue if the truth gets known. Her entire future reign would be marred by this episode and I don't want that for her. It would break her parents' hearts, as well as cause them great embarrassment.'

'Have you had a scandal before? You sound very knowledgeable.'

He looks at me sternly. 'The first lesson you need to learn, young lady, is to keep your questions to yourself. You're not supposed to have an enquiring mind; opinions are not a desirable trait in a monarch. Now, I suppose we should start with who is who in this family and household. At least then we can stop you not recognising those closest to you. But first, I shall make us some coffee. It is going to be a long night.' He plods over to the kettle while I sit in silence, thinking things over.

Sitting back down with our fresh coffee, enjoying a slice each of apple tart left in the fridge, I feel a surge of relief, as I tell him, 'Baptiste, I really do appreciate your help, as will Isabella when she hears all about it. Thank you so much. Are you able to show me around the palace so I know where everything is, especially where her Mother and Father's suite is?'

'Stop calling them Mother and Father,' he instructs me immediately. 'Isabella has only ever called them Mama and Daddy. This is the main thing that is striking them as odd about you. They think you're like a different person. Imagine that!'

It's daunting to realise how much I have to learn but I have to succeed. The repercussions if I fail are too awful to contemplate.

Over the next few hours, the King's Equerry fills me in on the basics of life in the palace. Walking on tiptoe and whispering, he shows me around, helping me to find my bearings. I try hard to take in all the information, worried that I may forget something important. We go around the palace one last time, he tests me on what I've learnt. I point out all the rooms I've been taught, and when I get them right, I begin to feel more confident that I can start to be believable and that I no longer need to hide in Isabella's room.

Baptiste gives a stifled yawn, then says: 'Very well, Princess, you need to get to bed; it's 4 a.m. The staff will be clocking on in an hour and we can't have any more raised eyebrows, now can we?'

'No, definitely not,' I agree, then impulsively give him a hug. 'Thank you so much for everything, Baptiste, and for keeping our secret. You've been the best friend anyone could ask for.'

The funny little man smiles bashfully before making his

way back to the kitchen.

My head feels like it's barely hit the pillow before Alix comes rushing in through my bedroom door.

'Isabella, you have to get up now!' she says breathlessly. 'Daddy wants to see you immediately. I swear I've never seen him so angry before. He's asking you to bring your credit card with you. If you tell me where it is I'll grab it while you get dressed.'

I feel a surge of panic at the mention of the credit card, something has clearly gone wrong with our plan. Was Baptiste right? Have we made a stupid mistake? I find myself hoping that Isabella is safe. It gave me peace of mind to know she had all the money she needed, but now I'm really worried.

'I keep it in the top drawer over there, where I've always kept it.' I try to sound confident even though I have no idea where Isabella actually keeps it - but I'm thinking since they are asking me, neither do they.

'No, it isn't here, there's nothing here at all.'

I try to look shocked, rushing over to the drawer to rifle through it. 'How strange. Well, I've no idea where it's gone. I must have mislaid it.'

My sister looks doubtful. 'I wouldn't bet on it,' she says. 'Seeing the expression on Daddy's face, I think they know exactly where it is.'

I quickly get dressed, drag a comb through my hair and brush my teeth before accompanying Alix to the King and Queen's suite. I take a deep breath, trying to stop my hands shaking before we enter their room.

As we walk in, the King is the first person I see. His face

is red, his jaw clenched and his shoulders stiffly raised up around his ears while his eyes fix on me angrily.

'You want to see me, Mama, Daddy?' I say innocently and see the Queen's eyes brighten at the salutation which helps me feel less nervous.

'It appears you're feeling better today, love.'

'Oh yes, much better now, Mama. What did you want to see me about?'

'We just wanted you to bring us your credit card, love. Are you sure you still have it?' The Queen glances at her husband and it's clear they already know the answer to this question. I feel my cheeks redden as I think quickly.

'Mama, it would appear that my card has gone astray but I know it can't have gone far.'

'Well, that's where you're wrong, Isabella,' the King booms, 'because your mother and I know *exactly* where your card is. It's with that street urchin you brought up to your room last night.'

I feel the blood rushing through my veins as I hear the King refer to me like that and for a moment I forget myself.

'Don't refer to her like that, Daddy. Take it back!'

He looks outraged. 'No, Isabella, I will not be doing that, because your so-called friend has stolen your credit card and she's been using it to stay at the most expensive hotel in the city. Now isn't that gratitude for you?'

'Sophia didn't steal from me,' I say hotly. 'She isn't a thief, Daddy, she didn't touch anything.'

'Oh, don't be stupid, Isabella! How then do you explain her having your credit card and using it to stay at the Palais Royal Hotel? She's been arrested and is currently in custody pending her court appearance in two days' time.'

'She's in prison? Are you joking? She doesn't belong in

prison! Daddy, please do something.' I think of Isabella, alone in a police cell, scared and not knowing what's going on. I'm the only one who is aware of her innocence yet I can't say a word. I rack my brains, desperately trying to think of how I can get her out.

The King is unyielding. 'I hate to break it to you, but the law is the law and it applies to everyone - including me.' His pompous attitude irritates me, and for a second I hate him for being so obstinate. 'That girl has committed theft and fraud. I know you wanted to help her but she took advantage of your kindness.'

'No, you've got it all wrong. She didn't steal it and it isn't fraud.' While it isn't strictly true, I decide to be as truthful as I can, saying, 'I hoped you wouldn't find out but I want to be honest because this has all gone too far now. The truth is, I *gave* her the card and she had my permission to use it. You see, Daddy, she was fleeing an abusive home; her father had attacked her and she had nowhere left to go. It was at the gate, that I gave her the card and told her to check into the Palais Royal. I wanted her to have at least one night where she could be comfortable and get a good night's sleep after what she'd been through. I promised her that no one would ever know and it was just until she was able to get her stuff and find somewhere safe to stay. If I hadn't, she would have been sleeping rough or worse - and I couldn't allow that. Can you forgive me, Daddy?'

The King's face visibly softens as my words sink in, while the Queen comes over to join me and puts a gentle arm around me.

'I see. That makes all the difference. I'm proud of you, Isabella. Privileged people like ourselves must always look after those less fortunate. Now that you've explained the situation I see that Sophia didn't do anything wrong and we'll make sure the police are informed so she can be released without charge.' His voice becomes firmer as he adds: 'You did a very noble thing, my dear, but in the wrong way. You just needed to come and speak to us and we could have helped in a way that wouldn't have landed you both in so much trouble.'

'I'm sorry, Daddy. I promise I won't do it again.'

'Good, well, off you go then and I'll see you again later.'

As I leave with Alix, my legs tremble but I feel an immediate sense of relief knowing that Isabella will be released from prison. It is short-lived, however, when it dawns on me that without her credit card, she has no money and nowhere to go.

As much as I don't want Isabella to experience my life, I know that Mireille would keep her safe. As I return to her room, I decide to get a message to my sister, asking her to collect me from the police station. At least then Isabella will have a roof over her head until we're due to switch back as planned.

The Pretender

Chapter 8

The hands of time no longer turn, for my concept of time was stripped from me the moment the cell door slammed shut.

I sit gingerly on the edge of the metal bed and place my head in my hands waiting for the tears to come: surprisingly they don't. In fact, not one tear drops from my eyelids. The knot in my stomach is making me feel sick. However, I quickly realise that this is not from a fear of being alone in this cell but from a fear that I'll never be able to find my way home again.

There's the rattle of a key and the cell door opens.

'Sophia Lazarus, it's your lucky day - you're free to go.'

I sit there looking at the policeman, wondering if it's another of his jokes. I don't move or react. Instead I just watch him, waiting for him to start laughing once again as he did when he and his fellow officer arrested me.

Sure enough – his comedy side reappears 'So, first we couldn't get you in here and now it seems we can't get you out. You're really free to go, *Sophia*. The palace has confirmed that Princess Isabella gave you the card and that you had her permission to use it. Therefore, no crime has been committed and you may go. My advice is to stop telling lies in future. Trying to pass yourself off as our beloved Princess Isabella was never a clever idea!'

I can't be bothered to even respond. I'm just so relieved at Sophia's quick thinking.

'Go on - scram or we'll arrest you for wasting police time,' he says gruffly. 'Your sister's waiting in reception to collect you.'

'Alix is here?' I wonder aloud. 'How does she even know where I am?'

'No, your sister Mireille. It seems someone tipped her off to come and get you. Looks like you've got away lightly.'

How dare he speak to me like that! I feel my face harden and my eyes narrow on the police officer until he begins to look uncomfortable.

'If you truly believe that, then you're the one living in Disneyland,' I say. 'You know nothing about me or my life, so please do keep your insolent comments to yourself.'

I see the policeman look down to the ground as I quickly brush past him to leave the cell. I sign for my belongings at reception then march out of the door.

'Sophia, wait!'

The policeman is beckoning me back to the reception desk.

'Your sister is waiting for you here.' I see him point to a tall lady with dark hair. She's painfully thin while her clothes are shabby and frayed, making her look older than her years.

'Sophia, I've been so worried about you! I thought you were dead when I heard nothing from you.' Her bony arms embrace me tightly and she kisses my cheek.

'Are you Mireille?' I whisper into her ear.

'Yes, of course I am Mireille. Sophia, are you all right?'

She obviously believes I am her sister. 'Did you bump your head? You seem different.'

'Maybe I am, Mireille, maybe that's exactly it.'

I see everyone in the room all look at each other as if I'm crazy before I once again stride out of the door and into the sunshine. At this point, I really don't care what people think of me.

I hear Mireille running up behind me, slowing down as she finally catches me up.

'Sophia,' she puffs, 'I really hate to see you like this. Please talk to me. It isn't like you to shut me out.'

'I'm sorry, Mireille, I just really need to get myself washed and into some clean clothes. That cell was so disgusting, I feel tainted. If I'm honest, I just can't talk to anyone right now.'

'I understand.' She pats me on the shoulder. 'Well, I'm here when you're ready. And you don't need to worry - I've persuaded Father to go and spend a few days at his friend's house. I've pressed all your beautiful clothes and put them into the wardrobe so that they're all nice and neat for you.'

'I have beautiful clothes?' I try to hide the surprise on my face but then realise that perhaps our idea of beautiful isn't the same so I try not to get my hopes up. But I smile back at her anyway.

'Yes, you know - the clothes you made yourself. They're all hanging up and ready for you when we get home.'

'Sophia makes her own clothes . . . wow, that's seriously cool.'

'Yes, you do, Sophia.' I see her eye me anxiously as I realise I've been thinking out loud again. I have to stop doing that but it's so hard to remember you're supposed to be someone else. I suddenly think how much worse it must be for Sophia not knowing the customs or oddities of my Royal life.

It's only a short distance from the police station to Sophia's family home in a run-down part of town that I don't remember.

I see the deserted play park that sits in front of the looming tower block. The ground is littered with discarded needles from careless addicts. I know there must be a lot of families that live here but it's clear why none of them would ever be able to use this park.

The lift doors are almost entirely covered with graffiti and hanging precariously off their hinges, forcing us to take the stairs. As we reach them the stench makes my eyes water. I pull my sleeve across my nose and mouth and pray that the flat isn't on the top floor.

'You certainly coped with that a lot better than last time, Sophia,' Mireille congratulates me with a tired smile. 'You're getting used to it.'

'How is it possible to get used to this? How can people live like this! I think I'm going to be sick.'

Why did I not know about places like this before? I feel a pang of guilt for the sheltered life I've lived. How could I have never known that this is how some people are forced to live? My life has been spent in a flurry of designers and privilege and never once have I ever seen that some people can barely eat.

'Trust me, a week from now you won't even notice,' Mireille says. 'As I told you before, it gets so much worse than this. You've just forgotten, while you were away at school.'

How can this kind of environment be healthy for children? For the first time, I feel ashamed of the life I've lived, surely my parents could have done something to help?

I'm relieved when we walk into the apartment. It is clean and tidy - probably thanks to Mireille, her face seems drawn and tired looking - and although it's shabby and sparsely furnished it's not as awful as I had feared, judging from the staircase.

'Here's where I've put all your clothes, Sophia. And here is where we keep the towels if you want to have a bath. When you're ready, perhaps we can have a chat. How does that sound?'

'That sounds lovely, I'd like that. Oh, I don't suppose you happened to see my phone, did you?'

'Oh yes!' she exclaims. 'Sorry, I forgot. I hid it because it was ringing off the hook and if Father heard, he'd have sold it. You know what he's like - he'll do anything for money. You go and sort yourself out and I'll fetch it for you.'

As I lie back in the water, my mind empties of all thought and worry. In the silence, it dawns on me that while this is not going to be an easy journey, nothing worthwhile ever was achieved without effort. An inexplicable optimism grips me. I know I'll be fine, no matter what happens. And I can compensate Sophia and Mireille for their help to.

Returning to Sophia's room, I look through the clothes in her wardrobe with growing amazement. They are, quite simply, stunning. She actually has a better day-wear wardrobe than me.

I pick out a cute little dress with a delicate collar detail. As I pull it over my head, I feel a pang of excitement at having met someone who can create clothes like this.

After getting ready I turn my attention to the phone now lying on Sophia's bed. I check and see that all her calls have come from a girl called Mai. I read through the texts sent and it's clear she's frantic. Not wanting her to worry I nervously call her back from Sophia's phone.

'Sophia!' she exclaims. 'Thank God I've got hold of you. Where the hell have you been? I've been absolutely worried sick.'

'Hi Mai, I'm really sorry not to have called you, but things have been a bit manic here. I've not had access to my phone and I've only just seen the calls.'

'Is it your father, Sophia? Has he hurt you again?'

'Yes, he did, but he's not here now. My sister persuaded him to go and stay with his friends for a few days which is good, but I had to leave in a hurry without my phone so I'm sorry I wasn't in touch before.'

'Thank goodness you are safe. Remember, Soph, if you need anything you just let me know and I'll be there for you. After what you told us about your father, I just knew something was going happen.'

'Thank you, Mai, you're the best. There is one thing you could do for me, actually.' I take a deep breath before continuing: 'You see, I hit my head and now I've got temporary memory loss - so can you remind me what I told you to see if it jogs my memory a little bit? The doctor said it might help.'

'Of course. Oh Soph, I don't like this at all. Please come to stay with me? I knew it wasn't a good idea for you to go home.' I can hear the tears in her voice. She's clearly a wonderful friend. Fleetingly, I wish I had a friend like that, but it's hard to get close to anyone outside the family. I'm only really close to Eddie, and Celeste's daughters Marie and Lucille. It's always been a struggle to find people who liked me for me, not just my title.

Mai runs through Sophia's life history for me, detailing the shocking violence she suffered as a tiny girl at the hands of her father, how she had won a scholarship to Notre Dame boarding school in Chartres at the age of seven and had only recently returned home after all those years. I'm shocked by what happened, but also in awe of Sophia and all that she's managed to accomplish already, despite the obstacles she's had to face.

As I bid farewell to Mai, I tell her not to worry if she doesn't hear from me, promising that I'll be in touch and that I'll try to call again soon. Switching the phone on to silent, I place it inside the pillowcase on Sophia's bed before I go to join Mireille in the kitchen.

She stops what she's doing and gazes at me. 'Oh wow, look at you - that dress looks great on you.'

'Thank you. I can't tell you how good it feels to be in some clean clothes again.'

'Would you like a cup of coffee?'

'Ooh, yes, that would be lovely. No sugar, please.'

Mireille looks surprised as she fills the metal pot with water and puts it on the stove. 'When did you stop having sugar in your coffee?'

'Er, I heard that you're supposed to start cutting your sugar intake by half so I thought I'd start there. I'm not sure I can bear to give up chocolate just yet though.'

'Just as well as I got these chocolate sables for you yesterday. They've always been your favourite, Sophia.' To my surprise, they are one of my favourites too.

Mireille pours out the coffee and passes it to me, before probing, 'What on earth did you do to end up in jail? I know you couldn't say too much on the phone but usually it's father I'm bailing out, not you. I was so surprised when

I got the message to collect you.'

I smile as it's beginning to feel as if Sophia is my guardian angel.

'Oh, it was just a misunderstanding more than anything. You see, when I left here, I ran straight to the palace - it just felt like the safest place to be. While I was there you'll never believe who I met.'

Mireille frowns. 'Who could you meet at that time of night? I'm not sure I like the sound of this.'

'I met Isabella, Princess Isabella herself.' It feels so odd to talk about myself like this.

'Never! Surely not. I can't believe it after all these years, after all the times I took you to the gates in the hope that you'd see her and you never did . . . and then you come across her in the dead of night. What on earth was she doing, roaming around the grounds at that time?'

'Well, between us, she'd been arguing with her father too. She needed to clear her head and so she went for a walk, and when she heard me crying at the gates she ordered the guards to let me in. She was so kind, Mireille. She took me up to her bedroom and we were talking away like we were the best of friends when the King and Queen came in. I was ordered to leave but on the way to the gates Isabella gave me her credit card and said I could use it because she knew I had nowhere to go and she suggested a hotel I could stay in.'

Mireille's eyes furrow as she struggles to take it all in. I don't blame her – I can scarcely believe it myself.

'I suppose I should have realised it was a bad idea but I was just so thrilled to be spared sleeping on the streets. The next day I was arrested because they thought I'd stolen the card and that I'd been using it fraudulently. Isabella confirmed the truth and I was let go. That's how it all happened.' I beam at her and take a sip of the coffee.

In truth, it was a narrow escape and I almost began to wish I'd never suggested it at all. But things are back on track now. And I still have six days left before I have to go back.

Mireille's face is flushed. 'I know they don't know you like I do but I can't help feeling angry that anyone would think my baby sister was capable of stealing.' She offers me another sable. 'I'm glad it's all sorted now though and you got to meet the Princess. What was she like? Does she look like you in real life too?'

'Yes, she does. In a lot of ways, we're just like twins. We seemed to have a lot of the same interests too. It was quite bizarre really, but in a nice way. I think you'd like her – and she'd definitely like you.' I can say that with absolute sincerity. I find myself really warming to Mireille, Sophia is so lucky to have such a lovely sister.

Sitting in the kitchen, sipping my coffee, I feel almost happy again, and the yearning I had in the cell to return home begins to subside.

Knowing how far we've come, I can't go home now and throw away a chance of a lifetime. I just hope Sophia understands when I don't return.

The Pretender

Chapter 9

It's been several days now since Baptiste showed me around the Palace, and I'm beginning to feel quite at home. The thought of switching back with Isabella later is weighing heavy on my mind, I'm going to really miss the Palace.

I sit down to the dining table, smiling at the other family members as we wait for our dinner to be served. The food I've had here this week has been sensational.

'My dear, we've some excellent news for you.' I see the King and Queen smile at each other broadly before they turn their gaze towards me.

Alix and Grace both look up from their melon sorbets, keen to hear the news too.

'What is it?' I ask with a sinking heart. In truth, anything the King and Queen thinks is excellent is unlikely to appeal either to me or to Isabella.

'Prince Frederick and his family are coming to visit us. We're hosting a state banquet for them - and we all know how much you two got tongues wagging the last time you were seen together.' The Queen's tone makes me blush despite the event not even happening to me.

'Mama, I don't know what you mean.' Her words make me uncomfortable but I see the Queen take my discomfort as a coy affirmation of affection.

'We've lined you up to do a joint royal engagement. As future heir to the Swiss throne he has a lot to learn, as do you, and it'll be so much more fun for you to learn the ropes together.'

'It sounds great,' I respond dully. 'When is it due to take place?'

'A week tomorrow, but don't worry, we're not going throw you in at the deep end. You'll have plenty of time to get used to the idea. Frederick is arriving on Tuesday so it gives him a few days to settle in too.'

Since the switch back is due to take place later tonight, it seems that everything is turning out just the way it was supposed to. Isabella will be able to resume her place here with no one any the wiser that she ever left in the first place. While I'm sure everything will be fine later, a sense of worry refuses to subside as I consider if something goes wrong.

'I'm really looking forward to it,' I tell them. 'Thanks, Mama and Daddy.'

I see the King look up at me in astonishment.

'Hmm, that's a surprise. I actually thought this news would send you into another meltdown.'

'I didn't have a meltdown, Daddy, that's a slight exaggeration.'

I see all members of Isabella's family divert their eyes down to their plates as smirks crease their faces.

'Well, Daddy, I'm really looking forward to it, even if you don't believe me.'

'I'm glad to hear it, and because we know it's your dearest wish to see Paris, we've arranged for your and Frederick's engagements to take place there. We've made sure there'll also be plenty of time for you to explore the city and enjoy yourselves, so it won't be all protocol and duty.'

'Oh Daddy, are you serious? That's amazing, thank you so much.' I can't think of a better time for Isabella to return, especially since I doubt she managed to actually get to Paris during the swap.

Then a suspicion grows in my mind. Why are her parents suddenly so happy to send Isabella to Paris - and why have they chosen to arrange a joint engagement with Prince Frederick? The answer is pretty obvious, and while they may stop short at arranging marriages these days, it appears they are still trying to influence the outcome.

'Daddy, answer me one question, please: why have you chosen to send me to Paris with Frederick? Are you hoping something will happen between us?'

The King smiles at the Queen before he replies.

'You and Frederick have been friends since you were children - and so why not?' He continues. 'We just thought it would be more fun for you to have someone of your own age to go with so you can enjoy Paris together. I mean, who would you prefer as a companion, Frederick or us, your parents?'

'You're certainly right about that, no offence! But I'm not sure I believe you. I can smell a rat, Daddy, and I think we all know exactly what you've both got in mind.'

'Mama, if Isabella doesn't want to go to Paris with Frederick, I will - he's gorgeous. I wish he'd look my way even just once.'

'Alix, don't be jealous. You'll have your day but you're only sixteen so you've all this to come.'

'I know, Mama, but I'm not destined to be Queen so it'll never be quite the same. We all know that Isabella has to conform to royal protocol. She has to get married, has to have children to produce an heir - but we're not that important, me and Grace, are we?' She looks away moodily.

'Don't talk like that, my love. You're all my children and your birth order doesn't matter to me. Isabella has a lot more pressure on her and that doesn't come from us but the public's expectation. We've only ever wanted you to be happy, and while we might think that Frederick is a good match for Isabella, it'll always be her choice as it will be for all of you.' The Queen speaks with sincerity as she seeks to reassure Alix.

As dinner comes to a close I retire to Isabella's suite. I love this bedroom, it's been my sanctuary throughout my time here. In only a few hours, this room will once again be occupied with its rightful owner and I'll once again have nowhere to go.

How is it that life can be so generous to some and so cruel to others? Why is it that I've been dealt parents like mine, but Isabella has been given a life of splendour, status and support? For a moment, I wonder if I'm jealous of Isabella and her life - but in my heart, I know the answer is no. I just wish that my life would get a little easier for Mireille and me. I'm so tired of feeling stuck with no idea how to change things. I don't need a Prince to save me, I just need a chance to save myself.

'Are you ready for your last night as a Princess?'

I look up to see Baptiste stood at my door; his friendly face has been a constant in this strange world and he has been my rock. In him I've found the father I always wished I had, for he truly has the kindest heart I've ever known.

'Yes, I am, and thank you for all your help, Baptiste. You've been an absolute angel to me and I'll miss you so much.'

Baptiste pushes his glasses up his long nose to hide his emotion, then clears his throat before saying, 'You're welcome, dear. Now, what will you do when you leave? Do you have anywhere to go?'

'To tell the truth, I think it's going to be down to luck - and do you know what? I'm OK with that. I don't know what's out there for me but I *do* know that I'll be happy one day, of that I have no doubt. The problem is, at the moment I just don't see how I'm going to get there. It feels like I'm embarking on a journey with no path and no map, with only my heart and soul to guide me. Does that make sense to you?'

'It makes perfect sense. The one thing you need to remember is that your past is finished and your future is not certain - so all you really have is the present. If you insist on living in your present and not worrying too much, I swear that you'll never go far wrong and you'll see that the future will work out in ways that you could never imagine.'

I hug Baptiste as the tears begin to gather under my eyelids. Then I sit on the edge of Isabella's bed, nervously awaiting midnight, the point when this fantasy ends and reality recommences.

As the clock strikes twelve, I sweep silently down the staircase, turning to look behind me at the Great Hall bathed in silver moonlight, just as it was the first time I set eyes on it. I unbolt the door at the back of the house and slip into the stillness of the palace gardens, each step taking me closer to the gates. When I reach them, however, Isabella is not on the other side of the gates, like she vowed she would be.

I wait and wait until the sky lightens with the dawn. Then, the tears that I'd managed to hold back pour down my face, and as I stand there at the gates watching a new day dawn, I realise they are not tears of sadness.

They are tears of relief.

Chapter 10

The palace clock chimes its midnight song, the faint echo rings through the darkened streets. I conjure up a picture of Sophia standing patiently behind the gates, awaiting my return. I toss and turn restlessly. I know I should have had the courage to return and explain that I just can't go back to my old life yet - but I just couldn't. I've let her down. Badly.

Wriggling down, I pull the bedclothes tight around my neck as I think of my family. I miss them so much! But I still want to experience life in all its beauty without the constraint of my title. That's the one thing they'll never understand. And it's the one thing that I can never have, as a Royal. Besides, I know they will still be there when I do return, but this may be my only chance to live life as an ordinary person.

'Sophia, are you ready? It's your big day.'

I wake with a start, not even aware I'd fallen asleep, as I open my eyes and see Mireille leaning against the chipped wood of the door. I can see just how much she cherishes her baby sister, her demeanour more of a mother than a sister.

'Yes, I didn't go to sleep until dawn with the excitement

of it all.' Today I'm off to Paris to be interviewed for the post of nanny to two children. It's a long shot as I've no professional qualifications or experience – but I helped Mama and the nanny to look after Grace when she was a baby. I've always loved kids so I hope that comes through. I have no choice but to try, I need to find my way to Paris.

'I've made you a special breakfast, you're not going to your interview on an empty stomach. I'm so proud of you, Sophia. It's a real step in the right direction and once you have an income and some security you can focus your attention on becoming a famous designer.'

I freeze. While I think it's great that Sophia has an obvious talent for designing, I'm absolutely petrified that someone will ask me to sew something for them and realise that I've never touched a needle in my life.

'Thanks,' I reply. 'I really want to be able to stand on my own two feet and we both know that I've got to get out of here as fast as I can. We don't want history to repeat itself.'

'You're right. I won't be able to keep Father away for ever, and if you stay here he's bound to have a go at you. It terrifies me. Oh, I know it's selfish but I'm going to miss you so much! It broke my heart when you left to go to boarding school. To have you back has been amazing. I just wish you could stay because I love you so much.'

I feel a pang of guilt and wish that Sophia was here to hear these beautiful and heartfelt words from her sister.

I suddenly have a thought, replying, 'Well, why don't you come with me? I mean, what do you have left here? You don't have a job to tie you down and I'm not a baby any more so I think it's high time you stopped putting your life on hold and started to enjoy it.'

I see Mireille's eyes widen in surprise and a flicker of

temptation flashes across her face.

'I don't know, I've never been to Paris. I might not like it,' she says doubtfully.

'That's true - but you might also love it. Mireille, look, you don't need to decide yet because I haven't even got the job. It's only a pipe dream at this point but do have a serious think about it. If I do get the job it'll come with its own accommodation so you wouldn't need to worry about anything. It really would be so exciting - and in Paris of all places. So, wish me luck, not just for me but for the both of us, eh?'

'Good luck, Sophia. I've no doubt at all that you'll get the job. I'm so proud of all that you've managed to achieve already, and if I didn't know better I'd think you weren't even part of this rubbish family. You're far too good for us, you truly are such a special person.'

My own feelings about Sophia echo Mireille's exactly. From our brief but momentous meeting, there is no doubt that Sophia, despite her hard life, is my equal - and now I've had the chance to walk in her shoes, it's clear that she's far more remarkable than I could ever hope to be.

'Don't be so silly,' I say. 'You're my family and to have such a loving and selfless sister means the world to me. I know we've had a lot of separation and you don't know me as well as you should, but if I get this job, come to Paris with me and we can make up for those lost years.'

I feel a surge of affection for Mireille that takes me by surprise. A few minutes later, I'm up and dressed and sitting at the kitchen table opposite her; warm pancakes with jam and butter, await me on the kitchen table. The small, well risen and fluffy spheres remind me of my childhood.

'I know pancakes were your favourite when you were

little,' she says, 'so I'm hoping that hasn't changed.'

'They still are, I can't tell you how much I love them.' As the smell and taste hit my senses it takes me right back to my childhood when Leonda would make banana pancakes from her family's secret recipe back in Jamaica. Every birthday, we would always request her pancakes. They looked a lot like the French version but they don't have any fillings just a sprinkling of sugar.

As the memory of Leonda fades it brings to mind Eddie. I see his cheeky face, his dark hair always cropped short. I see him working in the kitchens, helping out his mum, and looking utterly absorbed while I grew impatient waiting for him to come and play with me in the garden. Looking back, I can see how much he was learning from Leonda, he always loved to bake and cook just like his mum. In the end though his mother would always release him to avoid a tantrum from me.

Eddie has been living away in Paris for well over a year now and I miss him every day. There and then, as I munch happily on Mireille's pancakes, I decide that when I finally get to Paris I'll find the famous patisserie of his mentor. My sense of mischief likes that he'll have no idea it's me. If I pull my hair into a ponytail, he'd never expect that from me since usually I'd only wear my hair up for formal occasions.

As I prepare to leave for my interview, I take a deep breath to steady my nerves. This is such an important opportunity for me, I don't want to mess it up.

'Oh Sophia, you look amazing. I honestly don't know where you get it from; neither Manon nor I have your sense of style. Here, you'll need this for the train.' Mireille presses the last of her money into the palm of my hand.

'I can't take this, you won't have anything left! I'm sure I can find another way to get on the train.'

'I insist. I want to do this for you, to support you and be there for you – besides, this is for the both of us.' She gives a shy and hopeful smile.

I give her a big hug before making my way to the railway station. As the summer sun warms my body, I'm filled with the happiness of knowing that I'm following my own path in life. Somehow, knowing that I don't have the safety of my parents just adds to the excitement because I don't remember a time when my life hasn't been dictated to me through tradition and formality. Ugh, how I despise those words!

I think back to my earliest memories of being taught how I should act and talk, as if my life was nothing but a performance. I could never be myself. My life was not about choice but simply conforming to external expectations. However, now as I saunter through the busy streets, just another face in the crowd. I'm grateful that I'm now nothing to anyone except what I choose to be - and for the first time I understand what true freedom feels like and what it truly means to be normal.

The Pretender

Chapter 11

Red-hot droplets rain down on my skin from the shower, the discomfort strangely therapeutic to my troubled mind. What is it that I'm feeling right now . . . Is it anger? Is it sadness? Or is it fear?

No, it's not anger. I conjure up the image of Isabella in my mind and I don't blame her; this was her only shot at freedom and so I completely understand why she didn't return. And it's not sadness, no, not at all.

It's *fear* that is coursing through my body, making me tremble from within because now the stakes have risen in a way I was never prepared for. With the help of Baptiste I've managed to fool Isabella's closest family members - but under the intense scrutiny of the public eye and all those cameras and journalists, will the cracks be magnified to the point where the truth is undeniable? Just one mistake, one wrong word, could bring this precarious house of cards collapsing down around us, revealing me as an imposter – a pretend Princess - but also plunging Isabella into the greatest danger she's ever faced.

This isn't a game anymore, and the repercussions could be catastrophic.

Stepping out of the shower, I see that my skin is bright

red as I pull the huge soft towel tight around my body before walking into the bedroom.

'What on earth took you so long?' Alix says from my armchair, looking out of the window into the gardens.

'You need to get a move on. Frederick's here and he's waiting to see you.'

Unaware there was anyone else in the room, I recoil with fright.

'Sorry, Isabella, I didn't mean to scare you but Mama was so insistent that I come and get you, and you know what she's like.'

Still tense from the fright, I snap, 'Oh, for goodness sake, is there really such a rush? He'll be here for a whole week and he's managed however long without my company. Will another fifteen minutes really hurt him?'

Alix fixes me with a puzzled expression. 'Isabella, what on earth has got into you? When do we ever leave our state guests waiting? Mama told you last week, so you were supposed to be ready. Plus, you might find you're not disappointed when you do.' She gives a sly grin.

I start to put on my make-up before dressing. 'What do you mean by that?'

'I'm not saying another word. Just get yourself ready and then you can see for yourself.'

My hands tremble as I try to pick out an outfit before finishing my make-up in a way that still looks casual.

'How do I look?' I turn to Alix, waiting for her seal of approval.

'No way! What - are you going to the market? No, you're going to meet the Prince of Switzerland, and it's an official engagement. He isn't here for croissants, coffee and a girly chit chat.'

Alix disappears into the dressing room and returns with a smart green dress that falls just below the knee. It's a lot more formal then I would normally wear but still quite nice . . . the thick material belies that it's designer. I've never worn a designer outfit in my life.

I select a pair of patent black high heels to set it off - and I'm finally ready to meet the Prince. As I get closer to the State Room my nerves give way to excitement. The Prince of Switzerland! But this is Isabella's childhood friend so I can't afford to get this wrong.

'Are you ready, Isabella?' I see Alix smile understandingly as she leans in to give me a gentle hug.

'No, I'm terrified - but here goes nothing.' The doors fly open and, holding my head high, I walk into the room towards Mama and Daddy and the handful of guests assembled around them.

'Isabella, you remember King Theodor II, Queen Katharina IV and of course Prince Frederick who needs no introduction obviously.' My father smiles broadly at Mama.

I curtsy, say a polite hello to the King and Queen, then feel the weight of all eyes upon me as I turn to greet Prince Frederick. Gently clasping his hand, I feel a surge of electricity. Time stands still as I look into his large blue eyes; silently I trace his handsome but kind face with my eyes. His blond hair sets off his blue eyes perfectly as he stands in a navy suit and crisp white shirt, appearing more businessman than Prince.

'How have you been, Isabella? It's so nice to see you again'.

'I've been very well, thank you, Frederick,' I say stiffly. 'I hope everything has been well with you?' I see him smile and watch as it turns into a broad grin.

'Yes, I too have been very well, thank you, Isabella . . . but I must confess that I've really been looking forward to seeing you again.'

I feel my cheeks flush before giving a nervous smile. He's obviously taken with Isabella and I must make sure that I don't let myself get caught up in the romance of this situation. I'm not Isabella and the compliments and affection that he gives me belong to *her*.

'I must confess the same too, Frederick. I'm really looking forward to our engagement - I mean, our joint royal engagement in Paris,' I stutter.

'We're so pleased to hear that,' King Henri says with a twinkle in his eye. 'You're both heirs to your respective thrones so it's great for you to do this together.'

'I completely agree, Henri,' nods King Theodor. 'Much better than the stuffy way we had to learn - but the monarchy was a totally different beast back in those days. It's all so modern now.'

Their conversation fades into the background as I become submerged in my own thoughts. I wonder what the relationship was like between Frederick and Isabella. Does he think I'm distant? Should I be more familiar? Is he as nervous as me? Does he believe I'm Isabella, or does he think I'm a bit odd - that my behaviour is markedly different? As I ponder these ideas, I find that I do really hope that he sees a difference in me.

I want this Prince to know me and not just the person he thinks I am.

Chapter 12

Back in Fontainebleau after my interview in Paris, I look through the kitchen window at the bleak prospect outside – but not even that can dim my excitement as I end the call on Sophia's mobile.

'Was that who I think it was?' Mireille asks, her expression tense, twisting a tea- towel around one hand and then the other as she awaits my response.

I give her a sad look and sigh, then relent. With the broadest grin on my face, I sing out, 'We're going to Paris! What's more, I said we could leave today.'

The cloth falls to the floor as she launches herself across the floor to wrap me in her arms, the tears running down her face.

'Sophia, you're truly my saviour! I can't tell you how much I've dreamed about leaving this place behind and all the shackles that have made my life so miserable ever since I can remember.'

'Well, things are changing now, Mirielle, you can be sure of that. I didn't want to say until I knew I had the job, but the family I'm working for are one of the richest in France. When I asked them if you could come with me, they said of course – and that they could also help you find a job.'

'Are you serious? They would really do that for me? They don't even know me! Why would they do that?'

'They're business people. They're very well-connected and a good judge of character. If they recommend someone to one of their friends, it only serves to raise their standing even more. I'm sure they like to help too, but not many people do things for nothing in this world. They have their own agenda, as we all do.'

Mireille sits down suddenly. 'I just can't believe it. We're going to Paris and we'll have our own flat. Can it be true? Ooh, do you think it'll be a nice place – or will it be like this?' She gestures to the drab surroundings.

'My dear,' I say, putting on my best 'snob' accent, 'we're going to be living in the most exclusive suburb of Paris, in Avenue Foch, which is not far from the Champs-Elysees. To put it in perspective, if Princess Isabella went to Paris, that's the area where she'd be staying.' I try to keep the smile from my face; I just can't get used to referring to myself as a stranger.

'Oh, my goodness. I don't know what to say.' Mireille looks flustered. 'But I don't have nice clothes like you, Sophia. I'm not going to fit in; all my clothes have holes in them.' She begins to get upset.

'No problem,' I tell her. 'I'll pawn my phone - it's an iPhone 8 so that should give us plenty of money to get you some new clothes, get us each a new haircut and pay for our train tickets to Paris.'

'Oh no, Sophia, you can't pawn your phone! It was a present from your best friend for your eighteenth birthday and you've barely had it for five minutes.'

My heart sinks. I don't want to have to pawn Sophia's phone but I'm certain that she'd understand, especially if it ensured it got her sister out of the hell-hole they've called home for too long.

'Don't be silly, this is our new beginning and I'll keep the sim card, so as soon as I have some money behind me I can replace it.'

'Do you know, that's the nicest thing anyone has ever done for me. I don't know what to say.'

'Then don't say anything. It's the least I can do, and seeing you get out of here is worth far more than any phone.'

We make our way into the city centre, our first stop being the pawnbroker where I present Sophia's iPhone, box and charger.

'It's in great condition, and clearly has not been used very much so I can give you €900 - but that's the best I can do, I'm afraid,' says the woman behind the counter.

"We'll also need proof of purchase from you?" she continues.

"What? It was my 18th birthday present. If I wasn't desperate I wouldn't be pawning it, would I? If you insist, I'll just find the place where they have less scruples." I retort.

"Well, in that case I'll give you €850, if I'm not asking questions it'll cost you" she smirks.

'Fine, we'll take it.' I hand over Sophia's phone in exchange for the cash and we leave the shop in silence.

As the stores start to close and the sun begins to fade into the clouds, we make our way back to the flat.

'Mireille, are you going to tell anyone where we're going?'

'No, it'll be easier if we just go. I'll leave them a note so that they know we're not coming back. The truth is, I don't want to see my parents again and well if I tell Manon, she'll tell them, you know she can't be trusted. I've endured years of abuse and in that respect, I owe them nothing.'

'I completely agree with you there, so let's pack and get out of here. The quicker we are on our way the better.'

'Absolutely.' Mireille looks round nervously and whispers: 'I don't want anything to come between us and this opportunity.'

We hastily pack our belongings, my heart thumping with the fear that someone will come back, realise what we're doing and stop us. In half an hour, we're ready to leave. Stepping out of the block and leaving the Forest estate, we both heave a sigh of relief. If we can just get to the station without meeting anyone who knows us . . .

As we walk towards the station, I catch a glimpse of the palace and wonder what Sophia is doing in there right now. I've seen that she'll soon be in Paris conducting a joint royal engagement with Prince Frederick. He's a nice enough guy – I find myself hoping they get on well together and that he doesn't suspect anything. While there's always the fear that our secret will be exposed, I have complete trust in Sophia. The fact that she's got this far without being discovered shows just how much of a natural she is when it comes to royal life.

'Sophia, you look a bit pale,' Mireille asks concerned 'Do you want to go up to the palace gates before we leave?'

I realise that I've stopped walking and I'm instead gazing up at the palace, completely lost in my own head.

Giving the tiniest of sighs, I say: 'No, I just think it looks so beautiful and I'll definitely miss it when I'm in Paris.'

'I know you will.' She squeezes my hand. 'The palace has always meant so much to you, even from a young age.'

'Why do you think that is, Mireille?' I'm curious.

'I think you've always looked at the palace as a kind of

sanctuary. Those gates are designed to keep the masses out and I can imagine it feels pretty secure in there. Also, you've always had a connection with Isabella too. I suppose you've looked at her as a role model you never had in our parents. I think Father always sensed that you expected so much more from life than he and Mother had to offer. He always hated that in you. But, if I'm honest, Sophia, that's the part I love most about you. Call me biased, but I think you'd be twenty times the Princess that Isabella could ever hope to be. Her life has been too sheltered and pampered, so she's never had to face any challenges the way we have.'

I feel my cheeks burn because I completely agree with Mireille. The more I find out about Sophia, the more I admire her. By comparison, in my royal life I'm revered for a title bestowed on me at birth but one which I've done nothing to earn. It's people like Sophia and Mireille, the silent heroes, who deserve that reverence. These are the true leaders - but yet they will never be given the chance to show their greatness.

As we reach the station, I turn to bid a silent farewell to my childhood home and my family. Boarding the train, any lingering sadness is replaced by a flush of excitement and a sense of pride because I'm finally making it to Paris! The fact that I'm making it there off the back of my own hard work just makes it even more special.

Chapter 13

Walking along the platform with our entourage, I see the grey and black carriages of the royal train come into view.

The King and Queen kiss me in turn. Then Frederick kisses the Queen, and The King shakes his hand, saying, 'Now then, Frederick, make sure you take good care of my daughter in Paris. We hope you have a fantastic time. I already know that you'll both do brilliantly.'

'Thank you, sir. I will take very good care of Isabella, she's in good hands.' Frederick gives me a cheeky wink as the King turns towards the Queen.

'As if I couldn't look after myself, Daddy,' I say crossly. 'You should know me better than that.'

'Yes, yes, of course - but Frederick might have taken it as an insult if I'd asked for you to look out for *him*.' We all laugh, the King and Queen both have a good sense of humour and it is nice to see them both in such a good mood.

We say our final goodbyes, then board the train. The interior is tastefully decorated with dark furniture, light grey walls and cute little lamps on every table. In this moment, everything feels so surreal, as if I'm in a film. How does something like this happen to me? If only they knew my true background? Of course, my school friends were all from very wealthy families, but I'm not even aristocratic. I can't do this, I'm out of my depth. As my confidence deserts me, I want to rush off the train – but Frederick's voice interrupts my panicked thoughts.

'So, our adventure begins, Isabella. I really am looking forward to it - especially getting to spend some more time with you.'

His words cause my heart to flutter but I try my best to hide it.

'Thank you, Frederick – I'm looking forward to spending time with you too. And in Paris! It's so exciting.' My fears and uncertainties disappear as for the briefest moment our eyes meet. I'm afraid that mine will betray just how much I like him. He's not falling for me, he's falling for Isabella. Above all I need to remember that.

'Don't call me Frederick, to you it's Freddie. Isabella, you seem to have the weight of the world on your shoulders these days. You are so different to the girl I knew two years ago.' Frederick holds both his hands together on the table as he awaits my response.

I decide I'll tell him a part of Isabella's truth. 'Just lately Freddie, everything has felt very oppressive. I mean, I have all these responsibilities laid out before me, yet I'm only eighteen.'

He looks solemn. 'That's perfectly understandable. I remember well how it felt to go from royal child to adult and all the expectations that followed that transition.'

'This is my first major engagement and I feel so under-prepared.' He has no idea just how true my words are.

'Then just follow my lead. I've been doing this for a year longer than you so you're not alone - and if I don't know, and our advisers can't help - then we'll just figure it out for ourselves. I'd like to think we have a brain cell or two between us at least.'

'I'm just so afraid of letting my family and the public down,' I fret. 'What if I can't be who they want me to be?'

'There's your first mistake, Isabella. It's not the public who decide who you are. That's down to you. All the public want is for you to be genuine, to be understanding and to care. If you're able to deliver on all those things, if you make the time to be visible, then you'll never fail to please.'

I breathe a sigh of relief. 'You're totally right. I *can* only be myself. I can't let the pressure of these expectations take away who I am. I've been worrying myself sick.'

Frederick looks at me closely. 'I never had you down as a worrier, Isabella. You always seemed so carefree before – and . . . er . . . apologies for saying it but you never appeared to think too much about anything.' He bites his lip. 'I hope I haven't offended you?'

The fact that he's already noticed a difference between us brings a smile to my face.

'No, of course not. So, is that a good thing or a bad thing in your eyes?'

'I think it's a great thing. You seem a lot more genuine now - and I don't want you to take this the wrong way, but you also seem a lot more caring, in a natural way. I suppose we're all a bit more self-centred as kids.'

'You know, Freddie, I do feel like an entirely different person. Nothing about me is the Isabella you knew. So, I guess while we do this tour you're going to have to forget what you thought you knew about me and get to know me the way I am now.'

A sense of relief fills me as I find a way to broach this

subject with Freddie without giving too much away.

'That's the part I'm most looking forward to,' he responds. 'I can't wait to get to know this new side of you.' His kind words and attention make me blush.

A strange emotion grips me; this is all so bittersweet because I'm not the rightful Princess. Isabella will be back to claim her title soon and I'll be gone from his life without him even realising it. I fear that this situation can only ever end in heartbreak for me.

My voice chokes as I tell him, 'Thank you, Freddie, that's such a sweet thing to say. So, let's pretend that we've never met before and get to know each other as if this is the first time. What do you reckon?'

'That sounds perfect. But how can I get to know you properly if you're holding something back. Because you are, aren't you, Isabella?'

I blush and mumble, 'Not knowingly. Besides, you're a Prince - surely you don't want to limit yourself while you're so young?'

His eyes narrow. 'What are you saying? That because I'm a Prince I'm going to play the field?'

As I hear the words back, I realise how it sounded and try as I might, I can't find another way to express my fears. In the end, I simply say, 'Forgive me. I actually don't know the point I was trying to make.'

He stretches out in his seat and gives me a smile, running his hand through his hair.

'Just relax and don't think so much,' he counsels. 'Go with the flow and enjoy the ride, as they say. The direction of our lives is written in the stars - and do you know why that is?'

'No, I've no idea.' I confess, intrigued.

'Because the stars are untouchable and no mere mortal can ever interfere with them or rewrite things the way they would like them to be. I think I can talk for the majority of mankind when I say that we all would, if we could.'

'You're quite the philosopher, aren't you?' I tease him.

'Why, thank you very much, young lady. I'll take that as a compliment.'

While Freddie reads through his emails, I study my speeches and look once again over the itinery for our trip, excitedly noting all the places I will visit. Afterwards, I sit quietly watching the changing landscape skip by. In the silence of my mind I realise that I've spent so long trying to emulate Isabella that I've totally missed the point. The biggest mistake I've made is not being authentic. In truth, not many people on the world's stage know Isabella either, but if I'm not genuine and true to myself, it'll harm her reputation – and I can't let that happen, not when she's put her trust in me.

If I'm going to be convincing and pull this off, then I must stop trying to be a clone of Isabella. I need to find the confidence to walk her path but to walk it in my own shoes.

Chapter 14

As the train pulls into Gare de Lyon station an hour later, a sense of pride fills me; I've got what I wished for and I've finally made it to Paris. What would my parents think, if they knew that I was going to work as nanny? Daddy would have a fit. But this is the life that our citizens live, they need to work in order to support themselves so, why shouldn't I?

'Oh Sophia, we're here, it's like a miracle.' Mireille's eyes sparkle with tears as we disembark.

Before I can respond, I hear a commotion behind us and turn to see the family I'll be working for.

'Sophia, we're so pleased to see you again. You must be Mireille - we've heard so much about you. Welcome to Paris.' Monsieur and Madame De Castellane kiss us both on each cheek. The children, aged two and five, insist on Mireille and me picking them up so they can give us a big cuddle.

As Mireille hoists the girl into her arms, she says to the couple, 'Thank you so much for letting me come along with Sophia too. I'm so excited to be here.'

'Don't even mention it, my dear,' Yvette De Castellane assures her. 'The apartment is way too big for just one person anyway and you two sisters will be company for each other. I'm Yvette and this is my husband Marcel; this little rascal is my eldest Louis, and this little angel is my youngest, Elise.'

'Thank you for such a lovely welcome. I think you are two of the cutest children I've ever met.' Elise is put back in her pushchair and I take Louis by the hand.

Marcel gestures for a porter to come and put our luggage on a trolley, saying, 'We've got the car ready to take you to your new home.'

Yvette adds: 'We think you're going to love it - it's the perfect base from which to explore the city. It was our first home after we married so it has a sentimental value for us. Such happy memories.'

I feel nervous as I walk down the platform, can I really do this? Or will it all come crashing down and expose me?

'Have you girls ever been to Paris before?' Yvette asks politely. She is pushing the buggy and Marcel now has Louis riding on his shoulders.

I answer for the both of us, saying, 'No, only for my interview, and Mireille has never visited before - but I've always wanted to come and Mireille's the same. We're both so thrilled to be here.' I smile as I think of all the times I came to Paris with my family.

'Well, remember that you don't need to start with us until next week as the children are going to stay with their grandparents in Toulouse tomorrow. So, you can take some time to settle in and explore. If you don't mind, perhaps you could join us for dinner on Saturday night as we'd love to get to know you both a little more? Mireille, my dear, I don't know if your sister told you, but we may be able to help you find employment too. We have a lot of contacts and we're more than happy to help.'

'Thank you, that would be very kind,' she says shyly as her thin face lights up.

We make our way to where the Mercedes is parked, the chauffeur stands awaiting our arrival. Setting off through the city, our eyes are glued to the passing sights as our hosts chat quietly to their children. Driving around the Place de la Concorde – it's terrifying, vehicles race around like a rally track. I close my eyes as a speeding car looks like it's about to hit us.

We move up towards the Champs Elysees, and as we pass McDonald's I have to look twice, never did I expect to see that here. Carrying on past the Arc de Triomphe, we finally turn onto Avenue Foch, in my mind I thought it would be a quaint residential street but the road is wide and busy, as well as absolutely magnificent.

We pull up outside a grand-looking nineteenth-century apartment block. The concierge immediately emerges to collect our luggage as we follow the family into our new home. I know I'm used to living in luxury, given my true background, but when I look at Mireille, her dazzled expression warms my heart. It's lovely to see her so excited.

As the door to our penthouse apartment opens, even I'm astounded by how beautiful it is. The floors are marble and each room is spacious and well lit; the furniture and décor complement each other perfectly. There is a chandelier in the centre of each high ceiling. This is a home full of grandeur – I almost prefer it to the palace. As the owners of a chain of successful legal practices, I wouldn't be surprised if Yvette and Marcel were wealthier than my family.

'Do you like it, ladies?' asks Yvette, as the children run around mischievously.

'Yes, we absolutely love it,' I answer, as Mireille is so caught up in her own thoughts she doesn't even hear the question. 'Are you sure you don't mind us staying here?'

'Of course, Sophia - we want this place to be lived in. What's the point of having it if it's not utilised - and we need a bigger place now we have a family. Marcel and I don't want it going to waste and the thing we liked about you was that you seemed to be someone who would look after it. A cleaner will come in three times a week.' She looks up at the ceiling. 'We take care of the chandeliers as they are cleaned professionally, so you don't need to worry about them.'

'We will both look after it so well; it's such a stunning apartment and we truly are so grateful.' I respond sincerely.

'Good – well, we really hope that you will both be very happy here. If you need anything we are only up the road. There is food and drink in the fridge to start you off, and here's a little welcome gift for you both.' Yvette puts an envelope on the dainty side table, warning, 'Don't open it until we're gone. We will see you on Saturday for dinner, yes?'

'Yes, we'll look forward to it'.

We bid farewell to Yvette and the family, after which Mireille and I return to the sitting room. Quickly opening the envelope, we are delighted to see a beautiful card welcoming us to our new home: inside there is a gold credit card. The card explains that this is the credit card I'll use for any expenses relating to the children but that as a welcome present they wish to give Mireille and I €1000 with which to enjoy our first week in Paris. Never in my life have I felt so relieved. We would have had to scrape by and watch our remaining Euros carefully, but now we can relax and really enjoy Paris!

Never before have I experienced such extraordinary kindness, tears of relief fill my eyes as I realise the timing of this gift, just when we need it makes it so much more special.

'A thousand Euros!' Mireille shrieks. 'It's too generous of them. They surely can't be serious?'

'Look at it this way,' I try to explain. 'If you had more money than you knew what to do with, would you keep it all to yourself?'

'No, or course not,' she says. 'I just can't believe they would give us so much.'

'It's not a lot to them, it's just a lot to us as we have so little right now. And remember, I'll be taking care of their children, who are their most precious possessions. Their previous nanny left to have her own child, and they had real problems finding someone compatible with them and the children to replace her.' I put my arm around her. 'It's like I said: our luck is changing.'

Mireille's smile lights up her face, never in all my life have I seen such a beautiful and genuine smile. I feel a pang of guilt at the web of deceit I've had to weave.

'This calls for a celebration,' I decide on a whim. 'And I know just the thing. It's a surprise, so you wait here, Mireille. I'll be about an hour maximum.'

The smile disappears as an anxious expression reappears. 'You can't go on your own, Sophia; you don't know Paris at all.'

'How will it be a surprise if you come with me?' I say reasonably. 'Besides, I managed OK at boarding school, didn't I? In the meantime, why don't you explore the kitchen and see what we might have for dinner?' Hugging her goodbye, I take the lift to the ground floor and walk briskly down the hallway, opening the huge double doors that will take me out past the concierge's office and on to the streets of Paris once again.

I know where Eddie's patisserie is – it's on the Avenue Victor Hugo, which doesn't appear to be very far away from here. A fluttering of nerves unsettles my stomach. Despite the change of clothes and my shorter hairstyle, I'm worried whether he'll recognise me? After my family, he knows me better than anyone. I know it's a risk but I can't come all the way to Paris without seeing him, isn't he the reason I wanted to come anyway?

I find the patisserie, but it looks closed. I peer through the windows, trying to see inside, when a voice interrupts me.

'Good evening, Mademoiselle, may I help you?'

I jump slightly and turn to see Eddie himself stood right beside me, looking as if he's ready to go home. It's so good to see his face after all this time, but I suddenly feel terribly shy.

'Good evening,' I splutter. 'I was looking for a celebration cake for my sister. We've just moved to Paris and it's our first night. But I'm too late, you're closed.'

'I see . . . well, Mademoiselle, it just so happens that I made this amazing chocolate cake today for a customer who ordered it, pre-paid but failed to collect – so if it doesn't get bought before I leave I'll have to throw it away. I'd hate for my work to go to waste. So . . . how would you like to take it off my hands? It's complimentary obviously, for you and your sister, since it is a celebration. Do you like chocolate?' His eyes twinkle.

'Of course! It - it sounds perfect. Thank you. Are you

sure?'

He nods, giving me a strange look, then says briskly, 'Wait here, I'll be back in a minute.' He unlocks the doors and before I know it, he is back, carrying a large cake box. He gives it to me to hold before relocking the shop doors, then when he's returned he opens it to show me a beautiful cake created with all three chocolates – dark, milk and white. I lean forward and can smell the heavenly scent of chocolate.

'All I want in return for this cake is your name,' Eddie announces unexpectedly.

'I can do that,' I tell him cheerfully. 'My name is Sophia. What's yours?' I smile as I think of him seeing me as a stranger when we are in fact best friends.

'I'm Edouard Laurent but everyone calls me Eddie. It's nice to meet you, Sophia.'

Taking the box from him, our hands accidentally brush and I start to blush, clearly, it's as a result of this peculiar situation where I have to pretend to not know him.

'I don't want you to think I'm just chatting you up,' he goes on, 'but you remind me of a girl I grew up with. No joking, you two could be twins.'

'Really? Now that does sound a little like a chat-up line but I'll give you the benefit of the doubt. Besides, I think it's sweet. What's her name?'

'Oh, I don't need to trouble you with the details.' He pulls his shoulders straight before he says 'Sophia, I hope you enjoy the cake with your sister and perhaps I will see you again soon in the shop?'

'Yes, for sure. I've heard great things about this place, so I'm looking forward to coming back and trying something else. Thank you so much for this, you're a life-saver.'

I say goodbye then head back to the apartment. As I walk beneath the trees that line the Avenue Victor Hugo, I think back to the conversation I had with Eddie in the kitchen before my ball, how I asked him to let me come to Paris with him. While I have no intention of telling him the truth, a part of me would love to know his reaction if he found out I have done exactly what I said I would.

I wonder whether he'd be proud or whether he'd be mad at me?

As we watch the sunset from the French windows of our new home, eating the delicious chocolate cake, I reflect on what an amazing day it's been. I think about Sophia and how happy she'd be to know her sister is away from her wretched family home. For the first time in my life, I feel that I've finally had a dream come true - and I'm pretty sure that there's so much more yet to come.

Chapter 15

The orange glow of the breaking day streaks across the remaining night sky, I walk out onto the balcony, the cool morning air is refreshing as I ponder how I Sophia Lazarus, currently penniless and homeless could find myself in Paris with the Prince of Switzerland.

Looking across the Parisian skyline, my eye focuses on the Eiffel Tower to my right. I think about Isabella and wonder where she is and whether she is coping with my life and its pitfalls? Has she reached Paris – and if so, where in this city is she calling home?

My palms begin to sweat as I consider what is going to happen today and the risks involved. As much as I'm confident that we do look near-identical, Isabella and I are still from two vastly different worlds. It only takes one person to suspect the truth - and this whole plan will fall to pieces.

There's a knock at the door and I open it to see Freddie standing outside looking gorgeous in another dark navy-blue suit. In fairness, it is a colour that suits him well. Suddenly I'm acutely aware that I'm still in my pyjamas and haven't so much as brushed my hair yet.

'You're early,' I say. 'I wasn't expecting you until eight-thirty.'

A bemused smile crosses his handsome face. 'Isabella, I take it you haven't looked at a clock recently? I'm not early; it's you that's late.'

I glance at his watch and see that in fact it's almost 8.40 a.m. I've never been a morning person but the one thing that's becoming clear is that Isabella is.

'Oh no – I'm so sorry! Do come and sit on the balcony - it's an amazing view - and by all means help yourself to anything. I need to have a shower.'

Before I can scuttle away, I feel Frederick's hands rest gently on my shoulders as he holds me still for a moment.

'Isabella, just calm down. If you keep working yourself up about this then you're not going to enjoy it. At the end of the day, all we need to do is to be ambassadors for our families. We don't need to win a Nobel Peace Prize, we just need to genuinely support the places and people we're visiting, as well as lending our name to help raise awareness of important issues in this country and to foster good relations. Perfectly straightforward.'

I let out a long breath, then say resignedly, 'I know you're right but I just I don't want to let you or our families down. I know how much it means to them all.'

'Forget about everyone else. Instead, focus on yourself and on being the person that you are - and I swear you'll be fine.'

He's so kind it makes me want to cry. I smile back at him then dash off to prepare before the hair and make-up stylists arrive to ensure I'm camera ready. Slipping into a beautiful purple fitted dress, with delicate detailing around the neckline, I realise that this is what it must feel like to be a celebrity. I gaze in the mirror, struggling to recognise myself. Admittedly I look the part, but can I act it? While I've lived the family life of Isabella, I've just been a normal eighteen-year-old girl, but once I step outside to greet the public, that's when I'll experience what it's actually like to be royal..

I thank Sylvie, the hairdresser who, together with the make-up artist, Erica has made me look amazing. As I head off to find Freddie, I see he is sitting reading *Le Figaro* on my balcony and enjoying the morning sunshine.

'Wow! Isabella, you look stunning. You really know how to put an outfit together. That's a great colour on you.'

'Thank you, Freddie. Are you ready to go?'

Escorted by security personnel, I walk with him through the hotel lobby towards the entrance. The minute we step outside, a roar of voices and clicking cameras greets us. Immediately I feel disorientated and vulnerable. We are swiftly guided past the congregated paparazzi, each of them barging aggressively to try to get a picture of us, and into the waiting limousine before our motorcade makes its way through the Parisian streets. My heart beats frantically in my chest.

As we arrive at the venue I see rows of people lining the street eagerly waving flags, banners and trinkets; they are awaiting our arrival.

'Are all those people members of the public?' I ask.

'Yes, Isabella, they are all here to see us – well, mainly you. You really are very popular, the public adore you. At the front there, that's where the journalists and photographers can wait. Only a few are allowed at a time so as not to overcrowd the venue - that's why the ones who couldn't attend were outside the hotel.'

'Do we speak to any of those people, Freddie? I mean, if

they've made the effort shouldn't we also make the effort to engage with them?'

I see a smile creep across his face as he leans in and whispers, 'I'm sure we can go and shake a few hands if that's what you want to do.'

'Yes, I think it's only right. They'd be so disappointed to have come all this way to just be ignored.'

I think back to all the times I used to go to the palace gates with my sister, eagerly hoping that one day I'd get to meet Isabella. As I see the expectant faces and the children with their little flags with their proud parents behind them, I feel privileged to be able to make some children's dreams come true, the way I always hoped mine would.

In a change to protocol, Frederick signals that he will help me out of the limousine. He leaps out, walking round to open my door and offering me his hand to help me out. As I stand beside him, the noise of the enthusiastic crowd grows. I feel him take my hand in his, holding it tight, and a surge of confidence fills me. Despite my initial fear of the media I almost forget they are here because my focus is completely taken up by the masses of people who have come to support Isabella.

I think back to the conversation we had in her bedroom where she explained that she felt so stifled and trapped by her life - and I wonder how she could have felt that. Royal life can be difficult, true – but surely, it's the times like these that make it all worthwhile?

'Freddie, will you go to speak to people on that side of the road and I'll start on this side, then we can swap. Is that OK?'

'Of course, just stay close to your escorts. Now, are you sure you'll be all right on your own?'

I look into his eyes. 'Yes, I'll be fine.'

As I walk along the line of people stood before me, I shake as many hands as I can. A baby girl holds out her arms as if she's asking me to pick her up. Her mother raises her towards me and I lift the child over the barrier and into my arms. She gurgles and smiles, and I play with her for a moment and pose for pictures with the young mother before giving the child back and resuming my walk along the line, engaging with the onlookers.

Towards the end of the line my eye is caught by someone familiar. I look again - and recognise my sister Mireille! I see her lean over and speak to the person next to her. It's Isabella!

'Good morning, ladies,' I say in an inquisitive tone. 'Thank you so much for coming to support me.' I smile across at Isabella; a knowing glance is exchanged between us and I notice that she's wearing one of my favourite outfits. A black skater dress with three quarter length sleeves that I made myself.

'I'm so thrilled to meet you, Your Royal Highness, and can I just say how fantastically well I think you're doing. I know this is one of your first engagements but you're a natural. I think you're brilliant. I'm Sophia, by the way, and this is my sister Mireille.'

The crowds jostle us; my protection officer hovers close by with the immediate crowd eagerly listening to each word I utter.

'Thank you, Sophia, it means a lot to hear you say that. It's lovely to meet you too. Mireille, are you both from Paris?'

'No, we're originally from Fontainebleau, near the palace, Your Highness. We've just moved here for work.' Mireille adds shyly, 'We're exploring the city at the moment and loving it.'

As I look at my beloved sister, I can't believe she's the same person. Her hair has been cut into a stylish bob that accentuates her porcelain features and high cheekbones. It's clear she's put on a bit of weight and seeing her stood in new clothes, she looks happier than I've ever seen her before. She's a world away from the sister I left behind. I feel a wave of emotion as I realise what Isabella has done for her; that she's saved her from the home I always felt guilty for leaving her in. Tears begin to prick my eyes and I wish I could find a way to show Isabella my gratitude.

'It's been lovely to meet you both,' I say. 'I know that it's not exactly protocol but may I give you both a hug?'

I reach out and embrace my sister with all my heart. When I come to hug Isabella, I gently whisper into her ear, 'Thank you so much, I'm so grateful for what you've done.'

I resume my role and say goodbye to them both, catching Isabella's eye one more time before I continue to greet members of the public before re-joining Frederick. It's time to undertake our engagement as planned.

As I mingle with the most important Parisian figures, my mind keeps wandering back to my sister. I've never seen her look so radiant and beautiful. It's such a relief to know that she's finally away from our childhood home, that she can no longer be beaten by our father in one of his rages. She's finally putting herself first and not being treated as a slave by our parents as they succumb to the weakness of their addictions.

I'm touched beyond telling that Isabella came out to support me. Seeing her today for the first time since we switched, I'm aware that Isabella is no longer just a friend; in my eyes, she's become family to me because she's done something I would have struggled to do – she's rescued Mireille - and for that I will be eternally grateful.

Chapter 16

The warmth of the sun streams through my bedroom window, waking me earlier than usual. The temperature is rising even at this hour. I survey the sunny cityscape; a sense of accomplishment fills me as I realise how much I've actually achieved. It feels great to know what I'm truly capable of as a commoner, without the safety of my title to shield me. I just wish I'd been able to experience this without deceiving my family - but this is the only way I could ever have tested myself in a state of true anonymity.

I go into the kitchen to prepare breakfast - fresh fruit and my homemade pancakes, washed down with a jug of hot coffee.

Mireille walks into the kitchen to see my pancakes displayed on an oval dish, but they are already looking a little limp and soggy.

'That's a great first attempt, Sophia - we'll make a cook out of you yet.'

I grin and quip, 'I wouldn't pin your hopes on it.' I go to the cupboard and get out the apricot jam and as a treat some, Nutella.

'So, what's our plan for today?' Mireille asks.

As she pours out our coffee, I run off to my room,

coming back with a fold-up map of Paris which I lay out on the table, careful not to get butter on it.

'How about we try Montmartre first? I heard so much about it at school – about the painters who lived there, on the hill overlooking Paris as they produced their masterpieces. What do you think?'

'That sounds a great idea. I know it's very touristy there but I've always wanted to see the famous Basilica.'

'Hmm, now there's the difference between us. Never would I get excited about a church. It's easy to see which of us is the goody two shoes,' I joke.

Mireille shakes her head at me. 'I'm not a goody two shoes,' she says reaching for her coffee, 'and besides, it's a beautiful building.'

'Huh! I've had enough of them to last a lifetime.'

'What do you mean? Was your boarding school a beautiful building then?'

I feel the colour rush to my cheeks as I start to speak not knowing what I'm going to actually say.

'Oh yes,' I babble. 'Notre Dame was an amazing building with stained-glass windows and so on, but it was very draughty and freezing cold in winter, hence that's why I've had my fill of them already.' I really need to stop doing that.

'That's only one building, Sophia,' she says, 'so don't think you'll be wriggling out of it that easily. Ooh, I can't wait to explore and to finally know how it feels to be normal and carefree.' Watching as she slathers her pancake in chocolate spread. Indistinctly, she adds, 'I've honestly never felt as alive as I do since I've moved here.'

I cut a peach in two and pass one half to her. 'I can't argue with that,' I agree. 'We're finally free - and that certainly deserves a celebration.'

We emerge from the metro as I say, 'According to this map we just need to follow this road to get up to the Basilica. Although I think we should go off the beaten track and explore these side streets on the way there. It looks like it'll all lead to the same place eventually.'

'Perfect, Sophia, let's go for a wander.'

We stroll along the main boulevard, past shops displaying their mind-boggling range of products and tourist souvenirs. It's hard not to give in and splurge on mementoes. The narrow-cobbled streets leading up to the mount are enchanting, lazily we opt to take the funicular up to the Basilica to avoid plodding up the endless flights of stairs.

As the day melts away, we visit to Museum, detailing the illustrious history of Montmatre and the Moulin Rouge– after this we make our way to the Dali museum. Stepping through the door it's almost as if we've walked into Wonderland. The bright and nonsensical art that has come to define the surrealism movement is beautiful in the most confusing way. After the museum, we are in need of a rest and food. My feet are killing me!

'I have a good idea,' Mireille sighs as we sip white wine and finish off our caramel cream desserts. 'We should go to the Moulin Rouge for a show tonight? I know it's expensive but I think it would be amazing to see and it would be the perfect treat for us both.' I see her eyes sparkle with excitement as I agree.

I'm totally in favour of that idea, and after finishing up our coffee, we slowly descend in search of the Moulin

Rouge. Walking in silence, every step we take along the way brings another sight to be savoured. It's as if I'm walking in a dream. To be able to live in the very heart of the moment and in the very heart of Paris, is the most incredible feeling.

As we pause for Mireille to rummage around in the boxes outside the famous row of shops that sell incredible ranges of materials to dressmakers and fashion designers, I realise that *right now* I'm experiencing one of the best moments of my entire life.

No longer am I just existing but I'm living - and making some of the sweetest memories I will ever possess. And it's all thanks to the courage of Sophia Lazarus. How can I ever thank her!

Chapter 17

As we walk into the hotel lobby, silence embraces us. The shouting, camera flashes and commotion that have followed us around all day finally melt away and I'm once again alone with Frederick.

'Isabella,' he begins. 'Bella . . . I hope you don't mind but I've arranged a little surprise for us tonight. I . . . um . . . wanted to make sure we celebrated and that we did something special.' For once, he looks bashful.

'Of course, it's so lovely and thoughtful of you. I can't wait to find out what it is.'

'I look forward to it too. OK, so I'll come and pick you up from your suite at eight, and make sure you wear your best dress, alright?'

'No problem - I will, don't you worry. See you later then - and thank you, Freddie, for everything.' I mean it. Without him at my side, encouraging me, I'm not sure if I would have been able to get through today.

We give each other a final smile before we go to our rooms; closing the door behind me, I take a deep breath. I know that I'm supposed to be on my guard, I know that this can never work but right now, in this moment, I just don't care. I'm in love with him and there isn't anything

I can do to stop it so I might as well enjoy it - because the only thing I can be certain of is that this cannot and will not last. Perhaps the hardest part is that when Isabella comes back to reclaim her rightful place, Frederick won't even notice that I've gone. While my heart will pine for him; his heart will continue to belong to someone other than me.

The sudden shrill of the phone shakes me from my reverie and I dash over to the desk to answer it, hoping that the person at the other end is Frederick.

'Hello, love!' It's Mama 'Your father and I are so proud of you and how well you did today. The crowds absolutely loved you, and the way you engaged with them was so natural; it was as if you'd been doing it for years.'

'Thank you, Mama. It was so nerve-wracking, especially with all the media, it was quite intimidating to be honest. But I really enjoyed the public element of it. Truly, it was an honour to be there and to have that opportunity. I mean, where else would I ever get that chance? It was amazing.'

'Love, I can't tell you how pleased it makes me to hear you say that. It's only natural for you to feel constrained by your position at your age and to yearn for freedom. Believe it or not, I know exactly how that feels. For so long I've wanted you to see what a blessing it can also be, how proud you can feel when you learn what a difference you can make . . . but until now you've always chosen to view our fate as a curse. As your parents, it's been so painful to watch because we've only ever wanted you to be happy.'

As I hear the Queen spill out her innermost feelings to her daughter, a sense of shame grips me. What a web of lies we've created! Increasingly uncomfortable, I try to change the subject.

'Thank you, Mama, but wait - where is Daddy? It's not like him not to want to speak to me himself.'

There is a slight pause on the other end of the phone. I begin to think the Queen hasn't heard me, but then she hesitantly starts to reply.

'Daddy's been unwell, love. We didn't say anything to you before as we didn't want to worry you while you were away. He picked up a virus that's left him feeling a little breathless and with a nasty cough.'

As the Queen's words sink in, I stutter: 'Are you sure he's all right? Do we need to come back? Should I be worried?'

'Calm down, Isabella. No, you don't need to worry because he's going to be fine. It's nothing serious, but you may need to cover a few of his engagements when you return. It's probably best he's given proper time to rest and recuperate. He's not as young as he used to be.'

'Of course. Tell him I'll do anything just as long as he gets himself better.'

Oh no, never for a moment did Isabella or I - consider what would happen if there was an emergency. A niggling doubt lurks in the back of my mind. My hands shake as I put down the phone, picking it straight back up I dial my mobile number. It's a long shot but it's the only way I can think of to try and get hold of Isabella. It's no good. The automated message tells me this number cannot be reached.

I go to run myself a bath. Sitting on the edge, I watch the water-level rise; silently I pray that the Queen is right and that everything is going to be fine.

Slipping under the warm, scented water, I resolve that worrying isn't going to help. I try to put it out of my head and prepare for my evening with Frederick.

At the dressing table, I gently tousle my hair into place, adding a dainty crystal flower clip to one side to match my chic little pink cocktail dress. Sparkly pink shoes finish the look. Adding a spray of perfume and I'm done.

There's a knock at the door – can it really be eight o'clock already? Opening the door, I see Freddie dressed in his finest black dinner suit with his hands clasped behind his back regally.

'Bella, never have I seen you look as beautiful as you do now. This is for you.' Bringing his arms from behind his back he presents me with a blue and gold leather box.

'Oh Freddie, thank you so much.' I usher him inside the suite. When we're seated, I open the box to reveal a beautiful white rose corsage.

'I didn't know what colour dress you would be wearing so I went for something neutral,' he says bashfully.

'It's absolutely perfect. I couldn't have chosen any better myself.'

Freddie takes the corsage from the box and fastens it upon my right wrist. For a moment, no words are spoken; we just look at each other, lost in the moment.

'We'd better go, we can't be late.' Walking the short distance to the waiting car hand in hand.

The Paris landscape dances past the window of our Mercedes, as the Eiffel Tower comes into full view, sparkling with light. Freddie senses my excitement and grins.

'Nothing beats the Eiffel Tower at night,' he says kindly.

It's so beautiful - I've never seen such a romantic sight in my life. 'Look, Freddie,' I say dreamily. 'The tower is even taller than the moon, can you believe it?'

'When we climb it tomorrow, we'll be able to say we've been even higher than the moon,' he teases me.

When the car comes to a stop, Freddie comes around to open my door and help me out. We have arrived at the River Seine. Freddie grabs hold of my hand as we walk down the gangway of Pier 3, towards a beautifully illuminated cruise boat.

'Is this the surprise?' I whisper excitedly. 'Are we going for a cruise?'

'Yes, I hope you will like it, Bella.'

'It's the nicest thing anyone has ever done for me. I'm absolutely speechless.'

'Good. That's exactly what I wanted to hear. You're more than welcome, Your Royal Highness.' Tickling me surreptitiously, he says, 'Come on, Bella, let's get aboard before our dinner gets cold.'

The sides of the cruise ship are almost entirely made of glass, giving panoramic views across the river. In the bow of the ship, I can see a table for two set beneath the highest window, meaning we can look right up to the sky.

'Good evening, Your Royal Highnesses. Would you care for some champagne?'

As we nod our response, the waiter pours a generous amount into the crystal champagne flutes in front of us. We take a sip as the boat moves off from the pier.

'No matter what happens, I'll never forget this,' I say in a low voice, almost to myself.

'What is likely to happen?' Freddie asks. 'I'm not going anywhere. I'll always be right here for you. Hey, don't cry!' he says as a tear trickles down my face.

'You never know - just because we are royal doesn't mean bad things don't happen to us. But as far as I know, I'm not going anywhere either.' A heaviness comes to my heart as I say this, secretly knowing that soon I will be leaving this fairytale life behind.

As dinner is served, my nerves subside and despite every obstacle that lies ahead of us, I can't help but think that this is meant to be.

Chapter 18

It's 7 p.m. and our feet are still sore after finishing the last of our sightseeing. We have covered so much ground and even though we had a late lunch, Mireille and I decide to have something small before the show starts at 9 p.m. Since we splashed out on the tickets, we couldn't afford to eat there as well. So instead, head into one of the small restaurants near the Moulin Rouge.

'Do you want to sit outside?' I ask Mireille. 'I'm thinking that we can watch the sun set and eat our dinner and admire this beautiful view.'

'That's exactly what I was thinking,' she replies, 'and we can relax as we won't have far to get to the show. I'm so looking forward to it. What a glamorous way to end our first day exploring the city.'

We select seats outside and look through the menu. My eye is immediately caught by the baked camembert. Ever since I can remember this was my favourite cheese but I've never had it baked before.

'How do you feel about sharing the baked camembert? It looks so good.'

Mireille licks her lips. 'Yes, please. It sounds delicious.'

Sitting peacefully, we watch people rushing around

in the early evening, an interesting mixture of tourists and locals all outside on this balmy evening enjoying themselves. It's such a novelty for me to be around so many different cultures and nationalities and to see that we're all essentially doing exactly the same things, spending time with loved ones.

My chain of thought is broken by the arrival of our drinks and as this is our first night out in Paris, it seems fitting to propose a toast.

'Here's to us finally stepping out of the chains of our former lives. Here's to living in the moment and experiencing life as it happens and enjoying the ride.' I raise my glass of white wine to Mireille's.

We clink them together, saying, '*Salut*!' before taking the first sip. Never in a million years could I have imagined that I could be sat anonymously in Paris whiling away time on a summer evening in such great company. It truly is my dream come true and something that will live with me forever.

'Mireille, what is it that you want to do with your life, now you are away from home? Where do you see yourself going?'

'Ever since I was little I've wanted to have my own business to grow and nurture. But to do that I would need a certain amount of capital so at the moment it's not even an option I can consider. But if things changed, I'd love that.'

'I think you would make a fantastic businesswoman,' I reply enthusiastically. 'You are very level-headed and you truly have the most amazing inner strength. Two qualities I'd imagine would be essential in business.' I take her hand, saying impulsively, 'Don't spend time worrying about how things will happen. You never know what is around the corner and who you might meet or the opportunities that may arise. Miracles happen every day if you just keep an eye open for them.'

'I hope you're right, Sophia. I'd love to make something of myself and to turn my life into the polar opposite of our parents'. From an early age, I've felt like an outsider because we were always judged by their mistakes. You escaped, thank God, but for me it was as though my card had been marked since the day I was born. I want so much to break free of those judgements, but I just don't know if it'll ever be possible.'

'You are so much more than your upbringing and you *will* break free from your past. The process has already begun. As they say: "today is the first day of the rest of your life". I know that you will succeed in whatever you do - I have absolutely no doubt about that. As for those who have cast judgement upon you, that says more about them than it will ever say about you.'

It's too much for Mireille, who quickly wipes a tear from her eyes. Fortunately, our camembert is placed onto the table in front of us.

'Oh wow, Sophia,' she breathes, cheering up immediately. 'You go first and see what you think but watch out - it's hot.'

I break off a piece of bread and dip it into the hot cheese, allowing it to cool slightly before I put it into my mouth. 'Hmm . . . it's yummy, they've put other flavours into it and it's just perfect. Go on - try it for yourself.'

Mireille follows my lead and a look of bliss crosses her face as she wipes a rogue drop of cheese from her chin.

The air is still warm and balmy as we stroll down to the Moulin Rouge.

'I've never been to the theatre before. This will be my first time,' Mireille says.

'Let's hope it will be the first of many,' I tell her. Of course, I've gone to the theatre a few times with my family, but this feels so different – much more daring.

We take our seats and before we know it the curtains open to a burst of colour, sequins, headdresses and breasts. The outfits become gradually skimpier, with one dancer being clothed in nothing but her thong as she completes her routine in a tank with the help of two very scary-looking pythons. As the dancers move through their routines with electric energy it's impossible to keep your feet still; the infectious rhythms penetrate your psyche, none more so than the cancan finale.

Watching the dancers high-kick and squeal as they perform the cancan with verve, the way it's supposed to be. I can't help but think of the summer days of my childhood when my little sisters, Eddie and I would all attempt our own version - which consisted of kicking alternate legs up and down while turning our heads from left to right, with our arms around each other's shoulders. My smile is accompanied by a pang of longing as I bring Eddie once again to the forefront of my mind. I miss him.

When the curtain falls and we wait for the bus to the Arc de Triomphe, there's a restless feeling in my heart. It's not only the desire to see Eddie again; for some reason, my father's face keeps coming into my mind, and I'm left with a sense of uneasiness, mixed with guilt . . . but mostly it's fear I'm feeling.

Chapter 19

Today is our last day together - the day I must say goodbye to Freddie - and there's no way of knowing if I'll ever see him again. In some ways, I wish the truth was discovered, in the vain hope that he might love me for who I am, rather than as a Princess. Unfortunately, if this foray into this strange world of fantasy and tradition has shown me anything, it's that even if he wished to have a relationship with me, protocol and duty would make that impossible.

As we enjoy breakfast on my balcony, Freddie reaches for more coffee, our eyes catching for a moment. To my delight, I hear him say: 'Isabella, when do you think we might see each other again?'

So, our impending separation is weighing on his mind too.

'I honestly don't know,' I reply truthfully, and sigh. 'In a lot of ways, it isn't down to us, is it? Neither of us have the freedom to make these decisions ourselves, do we?'

'You're right; we both have our own engagements coming up so I don't think it will be possible for a while. Bella, I hope you don't mind me asking, but could we email each other in the interim? I would really like to stay in touch.'

'I would really like that too, Freddie. If I'm honest I've

been dreading leaving today, not knowing when I might see you again. Knowing we can write will make it a lot easier.' I smile as I realise I will have to create a fake email account, as I can't use my real one, can I?

'We make such a good team and we've grown so close. I don't want that to change.'

'Me neither Freddie. How well we get on has really taken me by surprise.'

Frederick moves closer towards me and it's almost as though we might kiss . . . but we both hold back and the moment passes. Perhaps it's wise, as we need to say goodbye rather than make things more complicated. Whatever happens now, I'll always have the memory of how I fell in love with my Prince in Paris.

On the journey back to the palace, I close my eyes and turn my head towards the window, I'm not in the mood to be disturbed. The clouds of negativity gently creep in, I feel tormented by my feelings. How could Prince Frederick ever love someone like me, even if he could overlook my background and my past how could he overlook the lies – the pretend Princess that he's come to know. We are from two different worlds and I knew from the start that it had to end one day – so why am I so upset now? This is the way it was always going to be.

From the moment, I first saw his face I should have known that this would end in heartbreak for me. Nothing was ever going to stop that from hurting like hell.

Chapter 20

Tomorrow I start my first ever job, as nanny to Louis and Elise De Castellane. This morning, as I drink my coffee, I've got the jitters. Can I really do this? Has it all been a big mistake? Then I think of the children. Louis and Elise are so cute there's no way I want let them - or their parents - down. We all had such a lovely evening for dinner, it was so nice to get to know them a bit more. Marcel and Yvette were so welcoming and kind that any timidity on our part - even Mireille's - disappeared in a moment.

Downing the last of my coffee, my mind turns to Eddie, whom I haven't seen since he gave me the cake. I didn't even go back to tell him if we'd enjoyed it.

At that moment, Mireille walks into the kitchen.

'It's my interview on the Left Bank today so I have to leave early. Wish me luck.' I notice she looks a bit pale. The holiday feel of our time in Paris is nearing its end, as we both prepare to face our responsibilities.

'Good luck - but I know you won't need it because you're going to be absolutely brilliant. You'll nail it.'

Mireille sits down to eat her breakfast. 'So, what's your plan for today?' she asks, dipping her croissant into her hot coffee.

'I'm not really sure. I might go for a walk.' My cheeks redden slightly as I know that walk will take me to Eddie's patisserie.

'That sounds nice.' She checks the new watch we bought her from the Galeries Lafayette the other day. 'I'm not sure what time I'll be back but if it's good news, perhaps we can go out for dinner to celebrate? If not, we can still go out - but it will be to that McDonald's to commiserate!'

'That sounds like a great idea, I'm starting with the children tomorrow so I definitely want to make the most of my final day of freedom.'

'It's a date then. I'll see you later.'

In the silence of the apartment, I try to think logically about something that has been plaguing me for a while.

Do I really have feelings for Eddie? If so, how long have I had them? Why have I never realised before that I felt this way? Does anyone else know? And is there any future for us?

Well, I know the answer to that last question. Eddie is the son of our head chef; I am the heir to the French throne. As a future Queen, I will have to marry a Prince. Frederick has always been their preference for me but as nice as he is, there is no spark between us. We get on well as friends but we could never be anything more than that.

Suddenly, the truth hits me: I don't want to marry a royal because *I don't want to be a royal.* The simplicity of it staggers me. The more my parents have tried to force me into the path of eligible princes, the more I've rebelled. Come on! I'm the only eighteen year old in the country who's even expected to start thinking about marriage. Most girls my age would be actively discouraged because they are too young - so why is it different for me just because I have a title?

The usual feelings of frustration rise within me. I jump up and run into my bedroom, picking out the nicest casual outfit Sophia has before doing my make-up and almost running out of the door towards the patisserie.

As I approach, I feel the nerves build in my stomach, making me doubt everything.

Am I over-dressed? Have I made too much of an effort? Will seeing him make me forget who I'm supposed to be? Will, I be able to maintain the rouse when I know him so well?

In truth, I just don't know - and now is not the time to be cautious. I'll never have the opportunity to explore things with Eddie to see if this can work, once I'm back in Fontainebleau - so it has to be now. I owe it to myself to know for sure before I return so I can decide what is best for me, not just what's best for the House of Bourbon.

I lean against the side wall of the shop, wondering whether I should peep in to see if he's there before I commit to entering. But then I think back to the last time I saw him in the palace kitchens, when he told me how terrible I was at sneaking up on people. The way his face changed when he saw me sticks in my mind . . . I've never seen someone look so pleased to see me.

Bracing myself, I push open the door and stride through into the shop. Eddie is there, busily icing a cake, so he doesn't see me to begin with. I walk towards the first stand, pretending to study the cakes. My heart beats loudly in my chest. I'm lost in my thoughts, waiting for him to notice me.

'Good morning, Mademoiselle, can I help you with anything?'

I turn to find Eddie standing behind me, wiping his hands on a clean cloth. Seeing the hint of recognition in his eye, panic rises in me that he might realise who I am. I quickly look back to the cakes.

'Mademoiselle, tell me - how did you and your sister like the chocolate cake? You are the same person who wanted a celebration cake, aren't you?'

'Yes, that's correct, we had just moved to Paris. Well, I start my new job tomorrow and my sister is having an interview today so I thought it was a perfect excuse for a return visit.'

'It does indeed sound as if you need something very special since it is a double celebration.' Eddie moves across to the other side of the room and brings back a pretty little round cake with a strawberry cream filling.

'I haven't yet had a chance to decorate it, so if you tell me your name and that of your sister, I will personalise it just for you.'

'Would you really do that? That would be perfect, thank you so much.'

For a moment I catch Eddie's eye, and the intensity of his stare makes me blush, yet neither of us breaks the gaze.

'Sorry, forgive my rudeness, Mademoiselle,' he mutters. 'I don't remember if I've asked you your name?'

'Yes, you did but I forgive you. My name is Sophia, my sister is Mireille - and you are Eddie. I believe that's what you told me last time.'

'That's a beautiful name, Sophia. You clearly have a much better memory than me. I'm sorry about that. I'd be more than happy to personalise this with both your names. If you take a seat, you can see how it's done.' He picks up a piping utensil and fills it with strawberry fondant icing.

His colleague is busy with a telephone order, which means we have the chance to chat uninterrupted.

'Thank you, Eddie, you're very talented.'

'That's very kind of you, Sophia.' He frowns. 'Did I mention before that you remind me of an old childhood friend of mine?'

Yes, you said we could have been twins. But you were very tight-lipped when I asked her name; I suspect you were avoiding the question. Was she an old girlfriend perhaps?'

I see his eyes flick down momentarily before he looks up at me again.

'No, she wasn't a girlfriend,' he sighs. 'We grew up in the same place so we spent a lot of our time together as children. It was a very happy period of my life.' He bends over the cake to concentrate, then says in a different tone of voice: 'Now, I don't want to talk about someone else when I could be finding out more about you in the short space of time we have.'

'Why a short space of time?'

'Because I'm nearly finished with your cake and I might not see you again.'

'Do you want to see me again?' I ask daringly.

'Yes, I would like to see you again; I'd like to take you out on a date.' I see how nervous he is as he studies my face for a reaction.

I smile as I put him out of his misery. 'Then I'd better leave you my number so we can arrange something. Perhaps you can show me some of the Paris sights?'

'That sounds perfect and I look forward to seeing you again soon. Don't say a word to my colleague but this cake is on the house too. After all, it is a triple celebration this time.'

I jot down my number on a folded cake box and we say our goodbyes. Excitement fills me and I can't wait to see Eddie again - but this time I won't be a Princess. I'll be a regular girl - and that's the best part of all.

Chapter 21

As the limo pulls up at the palace entrance, I see Isabella's family waiting outside on the steps. While it's only been a week, it's probably the longest Isabella's been away on her own before so I can understand why they are so eager to see her. Nevertheless, something about their body language feels wrong.

When I climb out, the Queen comes up to greet me, but she's not her usual self.

'Mama . . . what's wrong? Has something happened? Where's Daddy?'

'You had better come inside, love, we need to have a talk.'

My mind races with possibilities as I greet everyone else then follow the Queen into the King's office. For a moment, I wonder if our secret has been discovered.

'Sweetheart, we didn't want to worry you while you were away - but remember we said that your father was ill?'

'Yes, and you said it was nothing to be worried about.'

'That is what we thought at the time, but since then things have changed. Henri didn't appear to be getting better so we ran more tests which revealed that he has a serious heart condition. He's too weak for a transplant;

it's just not an option. Now I need you to be brave, my love.' She holds me tight for a moment before releasing me and forcing herself to continue. 'While we can treat the condition to buy some more time, it's incurable. Your father is dying, Isabella.'

Tears spill from my eyes; it's devastating news. My mind immediately races to Isabella. In an instant, our little game appears to have had the most devastating consequences.

'This can't be true,' I say, looking imploringly into the Queen's eyes. 'How could he be fine when I left but dying when I return? Surely this has to be a mistake. How about getting a second opinion? This can't be right!'

The Queen reaches out to wipe my eyes.

'I know you're upset, love, but this is no mistake. Your father appeared to be healthy but he wasn't; apparently, he's had this condition a long time but it just didn't show any symptoms until now. Isabella, you will be Queen sooner rather than later. Once your father dies, the crown has to pass to you.'

All of a sudden, I can't breathe. The choking grip of panic grabs hold of me, a fog of uncertainty and fear surrounds me.

'I can't do this! You don't understand, none of you understand!' I wail, escaping her arms as she tries to catch me. 'No, no, no, no - this has to stop now. This just can't happen.'

I run out of the office and up to my bedroom suite as fast as I can, jamming a chair under the handle so no one can come in. Alone in the sanctuary of Isabella's room I release a great torrent of grief. I cry out every frustration I've felt these past few months, all the pain of the past and my terrible guilt at being here as the pretend

Princess instead of the rightful one. I feel like a criminal and now who knows what will happen?

When I am finally all cried out, I know I have to take action. It's imperative that I find Isabella and let her know what's going on: we have to make the switch happen as soon as possible. She has to see her father before he dies.

But how the hell do I know where she is?

Suddenly, I have an idea. Sneaking down to the King's office, I let myself in and tap in the number of my best friend Mai. My heart is racing so hard I think I might faint. And then it is picked up.

'Hello, hello – Mai is that you?'

'Sophia! Oh my God, I've been so worried. Every time I've called your mobile it went to voicemail and now it says it's not in service. What's happened? Are you OK? You haven't had another fight with your father, have you?'

'Mai, I'm fine, thank you – and it's so good to hear your voice. It's a really long story and I can't talk now so I'll have to tell you *everything* that's happened the next time I see you. At the moment, I need a really big favour. It's a matter of life and death. You see, my sister is missing in Paris: would your dad be able to help me find her?'

'God, that's awful! What happened? How long has she been missing?'

I hate lying to my best friend of all people but I have no choice. 'She tried to protect me from our dad and he threw her out. I've heard she's in Paris but we're out of contact and I'm beside myself with worry.'

'Try not to fret. From what you've told me in the past, your sister is a very sensible girl. I'll speak to Daddy straight away and we'll come back to you the moment we have any news. Do you have a phone number we can call you on?'

The palace numbers are all protected, so I say hastily,

'No, I don't. I'll call you tomorrow at 7p.m. - is that OK?'

'Yes, that's fine. I'll speak you then. Oh wait, I nearly forgot: what is your sister's name, how old is she and what does she look like?'

'Her name is Mireille Lazarus; she's twenty-four, tall and very skinny, with dark hair cut into a bob.' I say my goodbyes to Mai and put the phone down, feeling weak at the knees. I thank my lucky stars that, through Mireille, I might have a way to trace Isabella. I sneak out of the King's office and back into my room. I feel a sense of relief that Mai's father will be able to help; besides no one has better resources then the police force.

My heart aches at how worried Isabella would be to know her father is so sick. Again, I rage against the injustice: why couldn't it be my father? No one would miss him, not even his own family. Life seems so unfair. I may only be eighteen years old but so far, I've witnessed two good souls taken while my evil father continues to go from strength to strength.

As I bring his vile face to mind, I make a vow to myself. Once I've switched back with Isabella, I'm going to work so hard to be the success I know I can be. While Mireille and I may have had the misfortune to be born into a cruel and dysfunctional family, I know that we both have a different fate then my parents. We have been blessed with the talent and, in my case, the will-power to break free from the shackles of our circumstances.

That's what my father has always hated about me – my refusal to give in. And as I lie here on Isabella's bed, despite the burden of my worries, I smile at how much I will relish his discomfort when he has to watch me become everything he was so scared I would become.

Chapter 22

As I set off for my first day working for the De Castellane household, I feel completely out of my depth. However, the truth is that my upbringing means that everything is out of my depth - and the only way I'm going to change that is to jump in at the deep end. Besides, I have no choice but to swim.

I'm well aware that I can't escape my destiny for ever, but this is exactly what I came for, the reason why I exchanged lives with Sophia - to experience being an ordinary French citizen. Many people will think a nanny is too lowly a job for a Princess, but the way I look at it, is that my future role as Queen will be one of service – so it fits in perfectly. What's more, I will serve my country whilst knowing how it feels to be a commoner - I shall, therefore, be able to rule *alongside* them instead of *above* them. I can imagine the look of horror on my father's face if he ever heard me say that . . . but I can also picture the pride on my mother's because in that way we've always been very similar.

Anyway, one day I'll have my own children so this will be good practice!

The family are waiting for me outside their house.

'Good morning, Sophia,' says Yvette. The children stand

either side of the couple. Elise stands beaming with her hair pulled into a little ponytail on the top of her head, in the most adorable way.

'Have you and your sister settled into life in Paris?' Marcel asks politely. 'You both seemed to be having such a lovely time when we met on Saturday.'

'We've loved every second of it,' I say with absolute sincerity. 'It really is such a wonderful city and everything I dreamed it would be. There is still so much to see though.'

Before the parents can respond to this, the children run forward and clasp their arms around my legs, rendering it impossible for me to actually move. I look down to see two beaming faces smiling back up at me with wide-eyed innocence.

'Come on, let Sophia go, you two. Louis and Elise are so pleased to see you; they have been speaking of nothing else. Let's all go inside and we'll run through the routine one last time.' Yvette picks up Elise and carries her indoors.

Marcel holds Louis' hand and steers him inside and closes the front door.

'It seemed better for you to start on a non-school, non-nursery day so you could have some time to get to know the children. The car is yours entirely, by the way. Tomorrow the driver will take you on the school run; Pierre knows exactly where to go so you don't need to worry about that.'

I follow Yvette through to the living room. As I sensed the other night when we came here for dinner, the house feels almost sterile and minimalist, lacking in personal items and the little bit of clutter that makes a house into a home. There's little evidence that any children actually live here. In some ways, I can really identify with the kind of life that these children have, as while they have everything money can buy them, it may be that fun isn't high on the agenda. As lovely as their parents are, with a chain of successful law practices, neither of them have a lot of time. At that point, I decide to put fun at the top of my list.

Marcel takes charge, telling me: 'So, the first thing you will realise about us is that we are not the kind of parents who impose lots of restrictions and stipulations, we are quite carefree that way. The only exception is that the children have a home-cooked meal each evening incorporating at least seven different vegetables as we have researched to quite a high degree just how much nutrition this brings to their diets. They do love fruit but we ask you to limit this to three portions a day as we try to limit the naturally occurring sugar.'

Yvette adds sternly, 'Under no circumstances may they ever have smoothies or pureed fruit as this increases the sugar to a very high degree. We do not permit them to have any chocolate or sweets but instead prefer homemade treats which are low in sugar. We've left you a list of suitable recipes. When you are more settled, feel free to let us know of any new ones and if you make a shopping list and hand it to us by Thursday each week we'll ask Pierre to get them for you over the weekend. How does that suit you?'

I try not to let my dismay show upon my face. I've only recently learnt to cook simple dishes with Mireille, and now I'm expected to make things from scratch and know the nutritional content of everything. As I blink, I feel the weight of Yvette's stare. She is waiting for me to say something.

Clearing my throat, I tell her, 'I'm sure that it won't be a problem at all. If I'm honest, I don't think I've ever cooked quite the way you want me to but I'm always happy to learn new things.' I knew I was expected to cook for the children but I thought it would be a lot simpler than this. I start to feel anxious and that maybe I've made a mistake.

'Well, that's to be expected as you're still young, but you're clearly a clever girl, Sophia, so I've no doubt you'll surprise yourself with what you can do.'

I smile gratefully at the support and encouragement. Thank heavens that I'm not expected to know all of this off by heart already. While I have no doubt that Sophia is a very clever girl, the fact is that I'm *not.* All the tutors in the world couldn't change this: my expensive education was a waste because I was never able to benefit from it the way someone else would have done. Luckily, I don't need to be a mathematician for my destined role perhaps that is the only thing I'm actually grateful for.

Chapter 23

I wake up in the small hours, in the silence of the palace. Despite knowing it was Isabella's choice not to switch back I can't help but feel responsible, as if I'm preventing her from being here. I jump out of bed to remove the chair that I placed under the door handle last night. Just as I've placed the chair back to its original position, Alix barges into my room.

'Oh wow, I didn't actually expect you to be awake,' she says. 'Papa is asking for you. Come on, throw on a dressing gown - he wants to speak with you.'

As soon as the words leave her mouth Alix departs as quickly as she arrived.

Fear grips me. What if I'm caught out? My reputation, everything about the person I am would be dragged up. I'd be humiliated and the damage could be irreparable. While Isabella has an equal place in the drama, I'm nobody. The blame would fall on my shoulders, I'd be ridiculed – The pretend Princess, the imposter. While I quickly put on slippers and a dressing gown, I pray that when I speak to Mai tonight, she will have some information for me. Isabella and I need to carry out the swap before the situation escalates any further. It's already gone too far.

Leaving the safety of Isabella's private suite, I walk down to the royal apartments. The King is propped up in bed and he's struggling to catch his breath. A nurse sits by his bed and adjusts the oxygen mask around his neck.

'Daddy . . .' I whisper. It's all I can say. For a moment, I forget that he isn't my father. In the time I've known the King he's been a strong and powerful man. True, he can be overbearing at times but his intentions have always been well meant. So, to see him now, lying helpless in bed and so visibly ill is frightening. It was only a week ago I said goodbye to him before leaving for Paris, when he was seemingly fit and well - and yet on my return I'm confronted by a dying man. It's too much. Tears race down my cheeks; I cannot stop them.

'Come here, my dear. I need to speak to you.' The King motions for me to sit next to him, and the nurse tactfully withdraws.

'I need to be honest with you,' he says, taking my hand. 'I'm dying; the doctors have said so. I dread the fuss, but we will need to make an announcement to the media soon as there's just no way to calculate how quickly things may progress at the end. When the announcement is made, you and the rest of the family will need to be prepared for what is coming, my dear. The coverage is going to be relentless.'

'Oh Daddy, no,' I moan. 'I'm not ready. I can't do this.'

He pats my hand in a loving gesture. 'Oh yes, you can. I've never worried about your ability to be Queen because I've always seen in you such strong leadership qualities. You've just undertaken your first solo royal tour and it was a great success. We are so proud of you. You don't need to worry, you'll be fine. This is your time to shine.'

'But Daddy, it's more complicated than you think. You

don't understand!'

'Oh yes I do, Isabella. Do you not think I was scared too? No one is prepared for the responsibility - and the expectation placed on them in a blink of an eye. It's a heavy burden and it's also terrifying. I do understand, darling. No one will ever understand more than me.'

The tears now stream down my face - the hopelessness of the situation, the guilt, all building up until I just can't hold it in anymore. I feel the warmth of the King's arms wrap around me, soothing me as if I was his child, stroking my hair and murmuring words of encouragement.

All of a sudden, he starts to reminisce. 'Do you know, Isabella, when you were born, the most vivid memory I have is of the first time I looked at your tiny pink face. It had taken us so long to have you; both your mother and I thought we would never have children, so to hold you in our arms was the most magical feeling. And then Alix and Grace came along – we were so blessed with you all. I remember thinking how proud it would make me to walk you down the aisle towards your future husband - the man who would make you as happy as your mother has made me.'

A tear escapes his own eyes.

'I can accept my fate but I just can't accept losing the chance to walk my daughters down the aisle on their wedding days. It breaks my heart to know how much of your lives I'll miss. It's so unfair. I would give up absolutely everything I have in a heartbeat just to have more time with you all - but time is the one thing I cannot buy. No rank or title will ever be able to change that. And in that way, Isabella, we're just like ordinary people.'

'I'm so sorry, Daddy,' I sob. 'I'm just so sorry.'

'Sweetheart, you have nothing to be sorry for, absolutely nothing.'

I sit there weeping in the King's arms, when a gentle tap on my shoulder alerts me that the nurse needs me to leave. As I leave the King's apartment, the Queen embraces me before going back to sit beside her husband. Scurrying blindly into the Kings office, I call Mai, even though it's very early. I have a renewed sense of urgency: the hope of finding Isabella as quickly as possible.

'Sophia, you sound awful, as though you've been crying. What's going on? Come on, I'm your best friend, you can tell me what's the matter is.'

'No, honestly Mai,' I say hoarsely. 'I've just got really bad hay fever, my eyes and nose are streaming.'

She's sceptical. 'Really? You never suffered from it before.'

'I know - it's weird, isn't it? This is the first year it's happened. How are you?'

'You won't believe it, Sophia, but I've been accepted into Oxford! I was so shocked. I'd got to thinking it wouldn't happen at all but I received the letter today.'

'Oh Mai, I'm so pleased for you. There's no way they couldn't have taken you.' Such happy news makes me want to start crying again. 'There's no stopping you now from becoming that amazing doctor I know you'll be.'

'Thank you, Soph. I'm so pleased you called. I really wanted to tell you first, even before my parents, as you've always been so supportive of me and my dreams.'

'I'm so proud of you, Mai. It really is a great achievement.'

'Thank you, that means a lot, it's your opinion that means the most to me. I spoke to my father last night and I'm afraid that so far, we haven't had any leads on your sister. There's been no paper trail for her at all. It's likely she's been paying in cash, since she hasn't been withdrawing money or using any cards. Daddy is awaiting information from the tax office to see if she's working and if any taxes have been taken. Do you know of anyone she would be with that we could contact?'

I can't mention Isabella, can I, because she is meant to be me? How complicated we made everything when we decided to switch places. Never could we have foreseen the consequences of our actions.

'No, I don't know of anyone else she would be with. I know she wouldn't have a bank account so she would only pay cash, although I'm not even sure where she would get the cash from. As far as I know she doesn't have a job.'

'Well, our best bet of finding her is if she does. She will then have to pay taxes and at that point we'll have an address for her - but at the minute we just have no idea where she is. I'm sorry I couldn't give you any better news Sophia.'

'Thank you so much, Mai. I'm indebted to you and your father. I really appreciate it.'

'Don't worry. Like I said to you, any time you need me, just call. Hopefully we'll have some more information soon. Try not to worry too much; I'm sure she's fine.'

I thank Mai and put down the phone, giving an unhappy sigh. None of us really knows how long the King has left, that's why it's imperative I get Isabella back as soon as possible and to make sure she can see her father before he dies.

The Pretender

Chapter 24

I walk through the door to the smell of dinner being cooked by Mireille. After my first full working week I'm exhausted, so to have dinner almost ready is heaven.

'You're an angel,' I tell her. 'I'm so tired I couldn't have faced even trying to cook, especially after the gourmet menu I'm expected to produce. I'm just pleased the children are effectively dustbins, so no matter how terrible it is, they happily eat it all up. They are just so cute.' I'm surprised how much I enjoying looking after Louis and Elise, we all have so much fun together that if they employed a cook, it would be perfect.

'When is it that you're starting your new job, Mireille?' I enquire. I smile as I recall her excitement to be offered the job of looking after the baby twins of the De Castellanes' friends. It was fantastic to see her beam with happiness, her maternal side never more evident.

'Not until Tuesday but I just can't wait. I love babies but twins are a little daunting.'

'You'll be fantastic,' I promise her. 'You know so much more about childcare than me. I just don't know what I would do without your advice.'

'Thanks, Sophia. I suppose I do have a lot of experience

as I practically raised Manon and you on my own. It was never the same when you went off to school. I always worried that you might never come back. I'm so pleased that you did, even after all these years.'

'I'm pleased too. It's been so good to get to know you again and see you escape that situation. I wouldn't have wanted to leave you behind. '

Mireille returns to the stove to check on our dinner. 'I'll always be so grateful to you for helping me to get out of there. It's as if a massive burden has been taken off my shoulders. I've never felt so free. Now, why don't you go and fill up those wine glasses while I dish up and then we can both enjoy the weekend. Do you have any plans for tomorrow?'

I pour out the wine, my cheeks blushing slightly as I tell her, 'I have a confession to make. I've met a guy and he's asked to take me on a date. So, we've arranged to go tomorrow.'

'Are you serious? That's terrific - I'm delighted for you. I hope he's nice though, I only want the best for my baby sister.'

'He's so lovely, Mireille,' I say dreamily. 'We've known each other for years but it's funny - I never looked at him as anything more than a friend and then *bam!* I wonder why I never saw it before . . .'

'Where did you meet him? We've only been here a couple of weeks now.'

'I didn't meet him in Paris, I knew him from school. He moved here for work.'

'I thought you went to an all-girls' school?' Mireille looks confused.

'Yes, that's right. What I meant was that his mother

was the cook at our school, so we met that way.' I feel my cheeks burn as I consider that this is almost true.

'Ah, I see. I hope it all goes well for you – You truly deserve to meet someone nice. I'd love to see you meet someone who took care of your heart. I think that's really rare. Perhaps one day I'll get to meet him. What is his name?'

'Eddie - and I'm sure that you'll get to meet him soon.'

She beams, raising her glass. 'I'll certainly drink to that.'

We chink our glasses together as I think about my date with Eddie tomorrow. It's crazy - how can I feel so nervous when I grew up with this guy! However, I can't deny that I am nervous.

At the end of the evening, I make my excuses and head to my bedroom, wondering once more if going out with him is the right thing to do. Is it fair on him? What happens if he falls in love with who he thinks I am? However, of all the things I can live with, regret isn't one of them. I fall asleep, wishing for tomorrow to come.

As the shop comes into view, I spot Eddie standing by the entrance, his head turned in the opposite direction. He shuffles from one foot to the other, putting his hands into and then taking them out of his pockets. I wonder if he would feel as nervous if he knew it was me.

'Hello, Eddie.' He turns towards me and I notice him check out my outfit.

'Hi, Sophia. Wow, you look beautiful. I love the dress. Have you had breakfast?'

'No, not yet.' I was too nervous to eat – not that I'm going to tell him that.

'Perfect. Follow me, I have a surprise.'

We hop on to a bus and as I sit down, I realise I have no idea where we are actually going. I feel a flush of excitement as I try to guess where I might end up. A few minutes later we are disembarking the bus.

'I hope you're not scared of heights,' he says suddenly.

'That depends - why do you ask?'

'This is why.' I feel Eddie's hands on my shoulders as he gently turns me around to see the Eiffel Tower ahead of us, its gigantic legs sprawl astride whole avenues.

'Are we going to the top?' I ask, a little nervous as I crane my neck to try to see as much of it as I can.

'Well, we can go to the top if you like but I've brought you here for breakfast.'

Is he joking? Bemused, I say: 'But surely they don't serve breakfast here.'

'Are you quite sure about that, Mademoiselle Sophia? Shall we go and see?'

To my surprise, Eddie bypasses the queue. As I wait for us to get into trouble I'm confused when we are beckoned over to the kiosk, where we are given instructions to follow one of the staff members. As we enter the private lift, we are escorted to a smart restaurant high above the city.

'One of my good friends is the son of the manager here and he was only too happy to help me make a great first impression. I figured since you were new to Paris, I should make our first date one you wouldn't forget.'

'I really appreciate the trouble you've taken, Eddie. I love it here. The view is out of this world. Thank you.'

'I get the feeling that you may be worth it.'

'I'd say you're an optimist for sure but maybe I'm just pessimistic about things like that,' I say cautiously. 'It's so hard to judge someone's character. If someone wants to hide something, they will.' I feel my cheeks blush with guilt as I say this and I look down at the menu.

'Now that surprises me, Sophia, I didn't have you down as a pessimist. You don't give that impression.'

'I'm not the kind of person who fits into a box. I'm a free spirit at heart. I yearn to be true to myself. I hate the idea of being chained down.'

Eddie looks at me closely. 'You're definitely an intriguing character. Do you know, there's something about you I just can't figure out . . .'

I smile coyly, not sure how to respond to that.

'OK, Sophia, where do you see your future taking you?'

'Honestly, I try not to think too far ahead, I prefer to live in the moment. I figure if I spent all my time thinking about my future, by the time I got there, I may have lost everything I hold dear in the present. I'm sure my destiny will find me; I'll end up exactly where I need to be.'

He looks impressed. 'Seriously, if I didn't know better I'd think you were the friend I grew up with. That's exactly the kind of thing she would say. How can two people be so similar, despite never having met before . . .'

At that moment, I wonder if I should confess but I stop myself, unsure how he would take it.

'"Now it's my turn to ask you a question, Eddie. Tell me a bit about your background. Do you have any brothers and sisters, are your parents still around, that kind of thing.'

'Well, since you asked so nicely, here goes. I'm an only child; my mother is originally from Jamaica and moved over to France to work in Raymond Blanc's kitchen, obviously she is an amazing cook. She met my father, he was French and they got married before having me a few years later.

Unfortunately, my father died when I was young and so my mother brought me up alone. She was able to get a good job as Head chef to a wealthy family, so I would play with their children while she worked.'

'Is that the family of the girl you talk about?'

'Yes, that's right. Mum and I were always treated as part of the family and we all grew up together. Although I didn't have any siblings, it felt like I did. It was a lot of fun and we are still close, we always will be.'

'If you don't mind me asking, who is it that you grew up with? I probably wouldn't know them anyway.'

The waiter arrives with our drinks and takes our food order before we resume our conversation.

'Actually, you would know her. I don't normally tell people because it can change the way they look at me. But I trust you, Sophia; I think you're different from the rest. I grew up with Princess Isabella. That's who I was referring to.'

My cheeks turn pink as I hear him utter my name. For a second I don't know how to react. I remain quiet and notice a confused expression cross his face.

'Oh my God, you grew up with Princess Isabella.' I try to react the way I feel I should and smile broadly before enquiring 'You were both obviously very close, given how you talk about her. What is she like?'

He thinks about it. I can tell he's choosing his words carefully, unsure of how much to say.

'She had the same yearning for freedom that you do, but that is not as easily achievable when you're a royal obviously.'

'Of course. As commoners, I suppose we take our freedom and privacy for granted. So, do you still go to the palace? Have you seen her lately?'

He answers quietly, 'Yes, I saw her a few weeks ago. She's a lot more settled these days; she seems to have taken my advice to focus on the positive aspects of her life rather than dwelling on the negatives.'

I smile and quickly divert my eyes as his words sink in. I really would have thought he'd have known me better than to think I'd be so easily fobbed off. However, it's reassuring to hear there's no suspicion so far.

As I sit with Eddie, the beautiful view from the Eiffel Tower laid out beneath us. I recall how it had felt like an impossible dream, to be able to visit him in Paris. Yet here I am, living that dream, with the person who means so much to me. How strange it is that a nation of people have fantasies about marrying a Prince or Princess. Yet, as a Princess, it's my dearest dream to just live a normal life.

If people really understood the constraints of royal life, would they think differently? It seems that you really do need to be careful what you wish for, as it may come true. After all, isn't a nightmare also a dream?

Chapter 25

'Baptiste, Baptiste, I need to speak to you immediately.' He looks alarmed but dutifully follows me to my room.

Before closing the door of my suite, I quickly check whether anyone has seen us. Once I'm satisfied we haven't been seen, I lead him into the dressing room and close the door behind us.

Baptiste's usual calm demeanour deserts him. 'Should I be worried, Isabella?' he enquires. 'This is such an odd display of behaviour; I don't really know what to think.'

'I have a confession to make.' I see his face fall, but I have to tell him the truth. 'Remember when you thought I had switched back with Isabella? Well, I didn't. She didn't turn up and left me in the lurch. I had no choice but to stay here and cover for her. I didn't want to tell you as I knew you would worry. But now the King is seriously ill and I *must* find her and bring her back. I've already tried but all my attempts have failed. You have to help me.'

He gives a heavy sigh before saying, 'I should have guessed that something like this would happen. Isabella is so tempestuous and headstrong. I should have anticipated that she wouldn't come back. Oh, Sophia: you've done very well- but I also think you've done enough. It's time we told the truth, it's all gone too far now.'

'No, no, no, please don't!' I beg him. 'We can't - I promised. If I'm found out, it'll taint Isabella's whole reign. Nothing she does will ever be enough to shake off the stigma. You know it'll completely undermine her credibility as Queen. Baptiste, you need to help me: I need you to go and find her so we can switch back without anybody ever knowing. Promise me you won't tell anyone. Swear it on my life and Isabella's life. *Please.*'

'I don't like this, I don't like any of this,' he grieves. 'How in God's good name have I found myself in the middle of this?' He mops his brow.

'That's why we need to keep it quiet. Work with me and we will find her and it will all end well. Look, I have a school friend whose father is the Police Commissioner and he has a team tracking my sister, so we should be able to find out through her where they are. I know they are in Paris because I saw them in the crowd at the engagement I did with Frederick.' I smile faintly as he comes to my mind.

'What's your sister got to do with all this? How do they even know each other?' 'Originally, Isabella was going to use her credit card to fund her trip to Paris, but then it got stopped. After the fraud charges were dropped and she was released, she had to go to my family's apartment on the Forest estate as she had nowhere else to go. Trust me, that would have been an education in itself,' I say bitterly.

Baptiste wrings his hands. 'Oh, dear God, just when I think I've heard it all. So how did they end up in Paris?'

I shrug. 'I've no idea. Isabella always said she wanted to go there but I'm not sure why. I've only spoken to her once quickly since we swapped when I saw her and my sister in the crowd. They both looked well and happy but I don't know anything else.'

'She thinks this is all some kind of game, doesn't she?' he moans. 'But it has well and truly backfired. The King is going to die and then she'll be sorry. She may have achieved her quest for freedom - but look at the cost. Just look at the cost . . .'

I take Baptiste by the hand. I feel a pang of guilt at seeing him so distressed as well as having to burden him with this again.

'Perhaps it wasn't the best idea,' I say gently, 'but I think she will have learned a lot from it - and maybe the experience will help her to become a better Queen. Having lived the life of one of her subjects, she'll gain insight and wisdom. So, you see it's not as bad as it seems.'

'I think we may have to agree to disagree on that, but you are right - as a matter of urgency, we need to find her and bring her back. Do you have any information, a place to start with?'

'Well, not an exact address but my sister has been seen on CCTV passing a certain place near the Arc du Triomphe most days. Do you think you could go there and wait?'

'So, you're sending me on a wild goose chase?'

I brush his words aside. 'Now, do you have some holiday you can take?'

'Yes, I suppose I do, but I can't go until Friday. I'm too busy. Can it wait for two days?'

'Yes, of course. Thank you so much, Baptiste. The King's illness is not public knowledge yet and he seems quite stable. If I find out anything else from my friend then I'll let you know.'

I cautiously open the bedroom door and shoo him out,

breathing a sigh of relief. I really do need all the help I can get, if I'm going to restore Princess Isabella back to her rightful place, ready to take her place as Queen after her father's death.

Chapter 26

It's the morning after one of the happiest days of my life and as I stretch contentedly in my bed, the memory of our fantastic date comes flooding back. However, as I realise that the line between us has well and truly been crossed I start to feel anxious.

What if this doesn't work? Will everything I've had with Eddie be ruined? Realistically, he doesn't even know who I really am - but if he did, would he feel the same? I think back to all the times we spent together at the palace, wondering if there was ever a sign of something more from him. Did I ever see a glint in his eye? Yes, I think so, but was he just being friendly? I mean we did grow up together. What if I'm making a big mistake?

Mireille taps at the door and sticks her head round it.

'Hi, Sophia,' she says, 'I've made you breakfast but I have to go out. I'll be back later if you want to do something nice?'

'That sounds lovely. It's my weekend off as the kids are spending it with their aunt.'

'Lucky you. I've left the paper on the table for you. I haven't got time to read it.'

'Thanks.' I smile as she heads out after which I lazily

stroll into the kitchen to eat my breakfast.

As usual, my breakfast is neatly laid out on the table with the newspaper folded up and strategically placed to the left-hand side. The more I get to know Mireille, the more I see that she's a bit of a perfectionist - but in the sweetest way. It's weird as I realise that she feels like one of my own sisters, the older and wiser one I was supposed to be.

I pour myself some orange juice and unfurl the paper. The headline almost screams at me, freezing me with shock.

KING'S DEATH IMMINENT

I re-read the headline a hundred times, trying to understand what I'm reading. How is this possible? My father has always been so well. No, this can't be true.

The article continues:

...

In an unprecedented move, palace officials last night announced that King Henri V is suffering from an incurable heart defect. His condition, despite the best medical help, has continued to rapidly deteriorate. Speculation on the King's health had started to circulate due to his long absence from the public eye. However, some had attributed this to the King raising the profile of his daughter and heir, Princess Isabella, who has recently undertaken her first series of solo public engagements. The nation has reacted with shock and sadness to the news. No further details have been given at this time.

...

I sit with my head in my hands, trying to take in the devastating news. Despite my shock, I know it's time I returned to the palace. For not only is my father dying but I will soon after be crowned Queen. How the hell can I get anywhere near the palace? How will I be able to get to Sophia without anyone suspecting? Suddenly, Eddie comes to my mind. I'll have to tell him the truth; he is the only person who can possibly help me.

Time ticks by but the shock refuses to subside, the only measure of time I can process is light and dark. I don't even notice Mireille walk in the door but she notices that something is wrong right away.

'Sophia, you look absolutely terrible. What's happened?'

Looking at her familiar face, tears come to my eyes and I realise that I need to confess to her too, as no matter how hard I try, I just can't get a grip on myself.

'Mireille, if I tell you a big secret, will you promise that you won't tell anyone? I mean *anyone*?'

Looking concerned, she sits down beside me, passing me a tissue to wipe my tears.

'Of course. You can tell me anything. I'm your big sister, remember?'

'But you're not. I love you, so much but you're not my sister and I'm not Sophia. I'm not who you think I am,' I say desperately.

'What are you talking about, Sophia? Of course, you're my baby sister, that's who you are.'

'Mireille, if I tell you who I really am, promise me that you won't repeat it. It's imperative that this goes no further.'

Fearfully, she promises.

'I've hated having to deceive you, and although I look like her, I'm not your little sister. I'm not Sophia Lazarus. My name is Isabella. Sophia and I switched places with each other the night she ran away from home.'

'Isabella? Isabella who?' Mireille looks baffled. 'Why on earth would you swap places with my sister? It makes no sense!'

'I'm Princess Isabella of the House of Bourbon – the eldest daughter of King Henri V and Queen Charlotte of France, and the heir to the throne. I know it sounds ridiculous, but I persuaded Sophia to switch places with me so I could have my freedom, and well, she needed somewhere to stay after your father kicked her out. Somehow, as ridiculous as it sounds now, it all seemed to work out so well. We originally agreed to swap only for a week, but then when it came to it I needed more time so I didn't return. I've been so selfish – I'm so sorry for the lies. Can you ever forgive me, Mireille?'

'Sophia - Princess Isabella . . . you're telling me my sister is in the castle right now pretending to be you? I'm so confused. I mean, we saw Isabella not long ago when she was in Paris with Prince Frederick: was that you or Sophia? Oh, my head is spinning, I don't know what to think!'

'Why don't I start from the beginning and go more slowly this time. The night that Sophia and your father had their argument, she came to the palace gates because that's the only place she felt safe. Ironically, that same night I had also had a bad argument with my father because I wanted to go to Paris. I was desperate for some freedom from my royal duties, but he wouldn't allow it'

Without meaning to, I smile at the memory. 'So, I knotted together my bedding and decided to lower myself out of the window and run away. It worked surprisingly well. I got as far as the gates when I saw your sister slumped on the ground crying. So, I took her to my room where we were talking about what had happened. But as I spoke to her, I couldn't help noticing how alike we looked. She said you had remarked on the resemblance too. On a whim,

I suggested that we switch for the week and she agreed. I think we'd both got to the point where we thought we had nothing to lose. In the end, my parents interrupted us which enabled me to just walk out of the palace gates and Sophia stayed there, pretending to be me.'

Mireille sighed. 'This is an awful lot to take in, Sophia – sorry, it's habit. I don't understand: all that happened months ago. Why didn't you change back?'

'Like I said, that was totally down to me. By the time it came to the end of the first week I hadn't done anything that I wanted to, so I didn't return. I felt awful knowing Sophia would have been waiting for me at the gates, but I couldn't go back then. I had no way of letting her know. I hope she wasn't mad at me about it.'

'How could my little sister be such a natural in a world to which she quite clearly doesn't belong? How has she managed it?'

I shrug. 'Who's to say that isn't where she belongs? I think Sophia will always be more of a Princess than I ever will. I'm just the one with the title. It hangs around my neck like a noose. I've always struggled with the fact I'm going to be Queen but I can't hide from it - and it's going to happen a lot quicker now my father is dying.'

'Who is dying, your father or my father?'

'My father, King Henri, is dying.' As I say the words aloud, I burst into tears, but I try to compose myself as I just don't have any time to waste. 'That is why I've had to confess to you, Mireille. You see it is urgent that I get back to the palace to see Daddy because I'll never forgive myself if he dies before I can say goodbye to him.'

'Well, can't you just call Sophia and ask to change back?'

'As a Princess you'd think I'd have everything in the

world but you need to allow for the fact that my father is both traditional and paranoid. My whole life has been tightly controlled; I'm not allowed a phone of my own. If I phone my parents, they'll just think I'm a mad person and block the number. There is no way for me to get a message to Sophia - but you heard me speak of Eddie, the guy that I saw yesterday? He's my childhood friend; his mother Leonda is Head Chef at the palace, and he's the only person I know who can get me back inside.'

'So that's it, he'll help you for sure.'

'Yes, I'm sure he will - but how do I explain that I've lied to him? He may not be as understanding as you have been, Mireille.'

'When you explain, as you did to me, he will totally understand.'

'Yes, I hope he will. I pray you're right.'

I sit in silence as a mountain of pressure weighs me down. How can I explain to Eddie that only yesterday I sat with him on a date pretending to be someone else? He'll be so angry at me for lying to him and who could blame him. Nothing I say will be able to take change that. I just hope he understands.

Chapter 27

I watch Baptiste drive away from the palace gates, heading for Paris. My heart beats faster as I hold on to the hope that we can find Isabella in time to do the switch. The King grows weaker every day; his skin has become sallow and his weight has dramatically decreased. Poor Isabella! When she does return, the father that she left behind will be almost unrecognisable.

Even though I'm not actually part of this family, I do care deeply for the King, as I do for everyone. Having spent as much time in their company as I have, it's hard not to form an attachment. At times, it has felt very overwhelming. I'm not keen on physical displays of affection. The way both the King and Queen are so fond of hugs is alien to me. When I look back, I notice how much I've shied away from physical contact during my life. The legacy of the violence I suffered as child. Only with Mireille, Miss Shaw and Mai did I ever feel comfortable hugging. However, being here has taught me so much: I've had a glimpse of how family life should be. It's been a truly wonderful experience. So, to see the King suffer this way is truly heart-breaking. *I need Isabella to come home!* I think as I pace to and fro, too restless to settle.

'Isabella, what are you doing outside at this time of the morning? Since you've turned eighteen you've developed some very odd habits.' The Queen ushers me inside and up towards the suite she shares with the King.

'How is he today, Mama?'

She brushes a hand over her eyes. 'We'll be lucky if he is here this time next week. This really is the end now for him.' She tries to compose herself, but sobs, 'Oh dear God, Isabella, I'm so sorry. I want to be strong for you all, but I just don't know what I'll do without him. He's the love of my life. I remember when we were young and everyone thought I'd married him because he was a Prince. But I would have loved him no matter what his place or position in life. No one has ever loved me or made me laugh like Henri; every moment we've ever spent together has been so special.'

'Let yourself grieve,' I counsel her, at this moment I'm the adult and she is the child. 'You're losing your best friend and your husband, the father of your children. It's fine not to be strong right now. We will help you, Mama. We will be strong for you.'

'Thank you, love, I just can't believe that our parting has come so soon. He's too young to be dying! And he's so worried about you too; leaving you with this burden at such a young age.'

'There's no use in worrying about it when it can't be changed. It'll only waste the time we've got left with him.'

The Queen rests her head on my shoulder for a moment; I can smell her familiar perfume and it makes me sad. Then she straightens, dries her eyes, and arm in arm we make our way in to see the King.

He's propped up in bed. His face is hollow and drawn,

and dark rings hang heavily around his eyes. His oversized pyjamas show how much weight he has lost in such a short space of time. Their marital bedroom is now a makeshift hospital with machines and tubes everywhere. His poor hand is almost covered with angry dark purple bruises from the cannula that's been inserted to give him fluids.

'Isabella, sit here with me.' His voice is a raspy whisper that is hard to hear. He beckons and I sit next to his bed, holding his hands in mine. The Queen stands watching, tears streaming down her face.

'Daddy, I'm so sorry to see you like this'. Tears fill my own eyes, the thought of Isabella missing her final moments with her father weighs so heavily on my conscience. It makes me wonder if I should just be honest but I know deep down that I can't. Baptiste was right: we've been so foolish. What were we thinking?

'The end comes to us all. Each of us has a different lifespan, and we can rarely predict the date of our own passing. If you're lucky, you'll live a long time but that's not the case for everyone. Age truly is just a number that way.'

He looks at the Queen and stretches out his free hand so that the three of us are all joined as he speaks.

'This is the end, Isabella, and that means your time as Queen is coming quicker than any of us could ever have foreseen. I know you've struggled and it's been such a worry to me, wondering how you'll cope. But over the past few months, there has been such a marked change in your behaviour that I am deeply reassured.' He manages a smile at us both, joking, 'If I didn't know better, I'd think you are almost enjoying the role.'

I smile back at him, for his observation is true: I've not felt this safe and secure since boarding school and I've loved every second of it.

‘I came to accept that you can’t outrun your destiny, Daddy, so it’s pointless to try. I really enjoyed the trip to Paris. That was a real turning point for me.’

‘What about Frederick, hmm? You seemed to get on well. As kids, you two played well together, but nothing more. However, there definitely seemed to be a spark there this time.’

My cheeks redden under the scrutiny of the King and Queen. I’m in no doubt that Frederick is someone I could love dearly – and for the rest of my life. However, the switch back with Isabella means I will probably never see him again. I’ve always known this would happen, but that doesn’t make it any easier.

‘Daddy, if I didn’t know better, I’d think you were trying to play match-maker,’ I tease him. ‘Freddie has such a lovely manner that it’s hard not to get on with him. Everything feels effortless when he’s around.’

‘That’s how it feels when it’s right, like it was with your mother and me.’ He gestures at the water and I put the straw in his mouth for him to drink from the glass. ‘My darling,’ he goes on once he’s swallowed, ‘I believe he’s the one for you - and nobody who had seen you together would think otherwise.’

The King’s face turns serious. He goes on: ‘Of course, if you do take this route there’ll be a very hard decision for you both to make in order to be together.’

‘What do you mean?’ I’m intrigued.

‘You’re both heirs to a throne. If you were to marry, then one of you must abdicate because you can’t rule in two different countries. So just be prepared that if he is the one for you, things may well become very complicated indeed.’

The King looks suddenly deathly tired.

'Well, let's not get ahead of ourselves,' I say, standing up and reaching over to kiss his cheek. 'I'm still very young and that's a bridge we'll cross if it comes.'

He struggles to speak, saying, 'I've never had any doubt that you would make a strong and independent Queen. Ever since you were little I've seen in you such a regal nature. Yet despite your royal status, you've stayed grounded in a world where you've never been able to move without a camera lens trained on you. Your best friends are with the children of our household staff. Not many members of a royalty would possess such a kind heart or the ability to treat others as their equal. In our world, we don't really have any equals because hierarchy is everything. I'm so proud to see that you didn't become a product of your background, you became better than it. You had everything, yet you remained so humble - and that's a sign not only of a truly remarkable Queen but of a truly remarkable person.'

'Thank you, Daddy. I'm so pleased you're proud of me, that means so much to me. We're very lucky to live in a world of abundance and opulence, yet thanks to you and Mama, we have been able to maintain the very essence of what it means to be a family. To the outside world, we are royalty but inside these walls we're nothing but family - and that is the best thing in the world. It's worth everything.'

Exhausted, the King falls asleep. Silence descends upon the room, apart from the gentle hiss of his oxygen mask which the Queen places gently over his mouth as the monitor continues to beep in rhythm with his heart. I say goodbye to the Queen and leave them alone. As I walk back to the room, I wonder where Isabella is, why she hasn't come back yet and if Baptiste is anywhere near finding her? Time really is running out, if we don't find her soon she'll never see her father again.

Realising that I need to prepare for the prospect of her not making it back in time, I decide to create a diary for her of the last moments of the King's life, so she can know the words he said to me but meant for her. That his words of wisdom will belatedly find their way to the right person. I feel a sense of relief knowing that whatever happens she will have the comfort of her father's words, that is the best I can do right now. I just hope it's enough.

Chapter 28

I hasten my step towards the patisserie, aware that it's nearly 11am and wanting to catch Eddie before he goes for his lunch. As the shop comes into view, I see Eddie just about to leave, seeing me he stops and smiles, waiting for me to reach him.

As I smile back at him my nerves intensify as I try to prepare myself for how he will react to this. Yesterday, I sat with him on a date pretending to be someone completely different! How can I ever explain that? Will my confession end our friendship for good?

'Sophia, what a lovely surprise. I wasn't expecting to see you.'

Eddie's beams as he bends down to hug me, giving me a gentle kiss.

'Are we able to talk?' I ask, 'There's something I need to tell you. It's really important.' My voice starts to shake.

'Uh oh, that sounds ominous. Is everything all right?'

'I'll tell you once we are away from the shop; we need to go somewhere we can't be overheard. It'll need a bit of explaining.'

I see his jaw harden and the smile leave his face as he ushers me into a small car park at the back of the patisserie, sitting down on a nearby wall.

I can't delay any longer. Taking a breath, I blurt out: 'I need to confess something to you and I really hope you understand and don't hate me for it.'

Eddie's arms fold defensively across his body. 'Go ahead,' he says steadily, but I sense his tension.

I plunge in. 'I'm not who you think I am.'

On hearing this, he doesn't respond, he just continues to listen.

'Do you remember when you told me that I reminded you of Isabella – you said that if you didn't know better, you would think that I was her? That's because it *is* me, I *am* Isabella.' He opens his mouth to speak but I rush on: 'You know how much I wanted to go to Paris and you know my father would never let me so I switched places with someone else who looks just like me - a girl called Sophia Lazarus. So that's why when I met you I pretended to be her. But it's been me, Isabella, the whole time.' Tears roll down my face, quickly I brush them away with my sleeve. 'I'm so sorry, Eddie, can you forgive me?'

There's a prolonged silence. The anticipation of what those words will be when they do come, makes me feel anxious and scared. Eddie looks stunned for a moment before his expression turns to anger. As much as it hurts to see him look at me that way, I can understand it, I have lied to him.

'No, Sophia, I can't forgive you. I honestly thought that you were different, that you wouldn't be blinded by my connection to the royal family. Clearly, I was wrong. But pretending to be Isabella? How low can you go! Do you think I'm stupid? Am I supposed to take you with me and tell the King this is his real daughter when I know full well she's with him in the palace *because I've seen her for myself*?'

'It's not Isabella, that's Sophia,' I say wearily. 'And yes, as a matter of fact that's *exactly* what I want you to do. Well no, not actually like that. I want you to take me to the palace so I can switch back with Sophia and see my father before he dies. Please, Eddie, you're the only one who can help me. Daddy must never know what we did, especially now when he's dying.'

'*Daddy*? Are you deranged, Sophia?' His voice has risen and I quickly check that there's no one around who can hear him. 'How dare you come into my life and treat me with such disrespect. I've done nothing to deserve this. Yes, I grew up at the palace and I'm good friends with Isabella, but that doesn't make me special,' he sneers. 'There's nothing I can do for you, Sophia. If you have dreams of getting to the palace to meet an eligible Prince then you can do it off your own back and not use me.' He stands up and starts to walk away, I run after him.

'What eligible princes are there, Eddie? Prince Frederick? We're just good friends, that's all. And I've certainly not met any others with whom I have a single thing in common. Besides, are you sure you're just friends with Isabella? Do you not think that there's something more going on there?'

'Oh, so now you're going to bring paranoia into the mix. Do you not think you are coming across as crazy enough right now without that? Isabella is the heir to the French throne, so I'm pretty sure she hasn't got any designs on me.' He looks back at me, it's clear he's really upset.

I need to think of something – quick. Something no one else would know.

'I get that this is a lot to take in, but if I wasn't Isabella then how would I know about the significance of my birthday cake. The butterflies because we used to chase them as children. How do you think I was able to find your shop in the first place? Because of the conversations we had about it. You knew how much I wanted to come to Paris because I asked you, remember?' But any hopes of convincing him of my real identity are quickly dashed.

'What are you - some kind of stalker? That cake was photographed and plastered over every magazine in the country, so don't come to me thinking that proves anything. Sophia, I grew up with Isabella. If she had pulled a stunt like this I would know about it because I know *her*. Now stay away from me or I'll call the police.'

It's over. I may never be able to get back to my family now. Eddie was the only person who could help me and even he won't believe me. It's my turn to get angry.

'I don't care if you think I'm crazy but mark my words: if I don't get to see my father again before he dies I will *never* forgive you. If my father dies, then our friendship and everything we had as kids growing up will die with him.' My voice deepens with anger. 'The first thing I'll do when I'm Queen, Eddie, is to get rid of you *and* your mother so I never have to see either of your faces again.'

Before he has a chance to react I run back to the street and back to the apartment. As soon as I arrive home, I quickly write a note to Mireille, my hands trembling, asking her to make an excuse to the De Castellanes; to explain my absence as a family emergency and offer my apologies. To let the children know I will visit as soon as I can and that I will miss them greatly while I am gone.

Feverishly, I pack up my clothes as I grab a taxi for Gare de Lyon train station. While I wait for the train that will take me back to Fontainebleau, despite it only taking an hour, it feels a world away right now. I rack my brains trying to find a way to get home, to see my father.

All I can do now is hope that the guards on the gate are willing to believe me.

As I sit on the train, my mind in turmoil, I feel so agitated. What if I don't get back to see Daddy in time? I mean, if Eddie, one of my closest friends, doesn't believe me - then who will? His words resound in my mind, the time he told me if I continued to chase my freedom I'd end up in a lot of trouble and here I am in the worst trouble of my life.

If the cost of my freedom comes at this terrible price, I don't know if I will ever get over it. How can I live with myself, if I don't get to say goodbye to my daddy?

Right now, I miss my family so much it hurts.

The Pretender

Chapter 29

'Isabella - Isabella! Wake up.'

At first I think I'm dreaming but as I open my eyes I'm startled to see the Queen beside me.

'What's the matter?' I ask groggily. 'What time is it?'

'Half-past three. Isabella, you need to come with me now.'

I start to wake up. 'Shall I get dressed first?'

'No, love, there's no time. You must come right away.'

My heart begins to beat double-time and tears fill my eyes as the Queen briskly walks me down to the King's room. When the door opens, I see the rest of the family, assembled around the King's bed. Alix is sat holding his hand; her eyes are bloodshot from crying.

'She's here, Henri. Alix, let Isabella sit there for a moment.'

I'm ushered to take her place, hugging her as I pass, and I in turn take the King's hand. His skin feels clammy and even with his oxygen mask he's unable to take full breaths without rasping for air; the deterioration from yesterday is terrifying.

'My darling,' he wheezes, 'your reign as Queen is almost upon us. On my father's deathbed he gave me his ring to wear throughout my reign so that he would be beside me with every step I took as King.'

In reverent silence we all hear him say: 'I shall now give you this ring, so that you will never feel alone as Queen. As long as you have this ring, Isabella, you will have me and I will be with you. I will never leave you. I will never leave any of you.'

The King has used up all of his small supply of strength: he's clearly exhausted. The Queen gently removes the ring from his right hand and places it in my palm.

In a voice thin and whispery voice, the King says: 'It'll be too big for you to wear but keep it with you and when you need me hold it close and rest assured I'll be there.'

My mind instantly races to Isabella, she isn't going to make it back in time to see her father. The tears well up in my eyes as I realise the enormity of what is about to happen. I place my cheek against the King's and kiss him tenderly as the tears spill down my cheeks. I do this, not as myself but as Isabella would, had she been here to say her final goodbye to her father. My heart breaking as I realise this is the end for the King, that his death is imminent.

'I'll be good, Daddy, I'll be the Queen you always believed I would be. I promise you that from the bottom of my heart.'

He can only smile.

The Queen now takes my place, softly singing to him the song they first danced to as man and wife.

Then she says: 'Thank you, my darling Henri, for being my husband and my best friend. When you leave me, I'll never again love another man because for me you are the only one. You will always be my everything. Will you promise me one thing, Henri? When it is my turn to leave this earth, will you be there to meet me?'

He has no more words left to speak but his eyes fix on his wife as a single tear drops down his cheek. As she holds him in her arms, he smiles beautifully at her one last time - and takes his final breath.

The room falls silent. No one speaks for what seems like an eternity. We all stand there and gaze at the Queen, still holding her husband in her arms.

She sheds no tears; her calmness is almost eerie. At first, I wonder if she realises that he's dead. We all look at one another, debating whether we should say something - but we don't; we leave her in the peace of the moment.

Finally, she releases the King and turns to us, the grief etched across her face. We all go to her, hugging each other in consolation.

Suddenly the door opens, and the palace doctor enters the room to check for signs of life, certifying the time of death as 4.09 a.m.

'I'm so sorry for your loss, Your Royal Highnesses,' he says in a sombre voice, then silently retreats from the room.

We all leave the King's room, when a hand suddenly clutches mine. I turn to see the Queen. A small smile crosses her lips.

'Isabella, come with me.'

Confused and still traumatised, I follow the Queen, Alix and Grace into the State Room, where all the household staff have been assembled. The Queen leads me to the middle of the room before stepping back to where the others are standing. No words are spoken. I feel a hundred eyes on me but I've no idea why. Suddenly, two strange men march in. The crowd parts to let them through and they walk straight up to me before producing a scroll from which they read:

'Our Almighty God in His mercy has called our late Sovereign Lord King Henri V to His service. The royal crown is solely and rightfully bestowed upon the High and Mighty Princess Isabella Catherine Violette Bourbon. The Lords Spiritual and Temporal of this realm, being here assisted with these His late Majesty's Privy Council, do now publish and proclaim that the High and Mighty Princess Isabella Catherine Violette is now, by the death of our late sovereign, to become Queen Isabella II of France. She will be Queen of this realm and all other realms and territories. By the Grace of God by whom all Kings and Queens do reign, bless the Royal Princess Isabella with long and happy years to reign over us.'

The men drop to their knees before me and lower their heads, and the rest of the room follows suit.

'The King is dead, long live the Queen!' is chanted in unison three times, ringing high up into the rafters of the enormous room.

As I stand there in my pyjamas and dressing gown, my hair unbrushed and with sleep still in my eyes, it feels as if I'm part of some ridiculous dream from which I am about to emerge. But no, this is real life. By a twist of fate, I, Sophia Lazarus, daughter to two substance dependant parents, born in the notorious Forest estate and beaten black and blue, have stood in the shoes of a royal Princess and am now being hailed as Queen of France.

'May I go back to bed now?' I hear myself say, the assembled crowd all burst out laughing at my response. I watch as the Queen, Alix and Grace all stand smiling before me. Even in the midst of this tragedy it is nice to see them smile.

'Of course, mam,' one of the men says respectfully. 'Would you like to review the announcement of the King's death before it's released?'

'No, I think the Queen would like to do that.'

She curtseys to me, saying, 'Thank you, Queen Isabella II. I'd like that very much.'

'Thank you, Mama, thank you to everyone,' I manage to say. 'Let's all get some sleep and we can start afresh in the morning.'

I retire to my bedroom but no matter how hard I try I just can't sleep. The crazy series of events replay in my mind – quickly I jot down the last words spoken by the King before I forget. After which I place the journal and the ring in the bedside cabinet for Isabella when she eventually returns.

The Pretender

Chapter 30

My father is dead – my heart breaks into a million pieces as I stand staring at the announcement.

'Dreadful news about the King, isn't it,' chatters the lady behind the newspaper stand. 'Poor Isabella, such a lot of responsibility at such a young age. It hardly seems fair on her, becoming Queen and dealing with the grief of losing her father too. Let's hope that Frederick comes back. He'll be a rock for her, that's for sure. That'll be one Euro fifty please, dear.'

As she gives me the fifty cents change, she goes on, 'Yes, I saw the photos of them saying goodbye at the Gare de Lyons up in Paris. They already looked like a proper couple - and a lovely one at that.'

I smile weakly and thank the lady as I take the paper to the park behind the palace. Perching on the edge of the fountain, I look over at my family home, the place that felt like a prison to me but now feels like an impenetrable fortress.

Unfurling the paper, I see my father's face and read the announcement of his death.

It is with deepest sadness that the Palace can confirm that King Henri V died this morning at 4.09 a.m. surrounded by his family. No further details are available at this time but details of the late King's funeral will be released in due course.

How could he have been surrounded by his family when I'm sat right here! He died not realising that I had left, that the person with him wasn't me. How I wish I could have told him how much I loved him, how sorry I was - but above all to have heard his voice just one more time. How could I have predicted, the day I so happily left the palace behind, what the consequences would be? How could I have known that the night I changed lives with Sophia was the last time I would ever see my father again. I will never blame her: this is entirely my own fault.

What I would give to be able to turn the clock back, to make sure I returned after that week, like we planned. Had I known then what I know now, I would never have chosen to stay away so long. How can I ever get over this? How can I ever forgive myself?

Crowds of people are gathered outside the palace gates, laying flowers and weeping. Shedding tears for a man they never knew, they have never met. And yet here I am, his first-born daughter and their rightful Queen, stood amongst them. If I said that now to them, they would all look at me like I was crazy. What a fickle world we live in, when seeing has to be believing. Although, isn't that what I was seeking, to be normal and here I am outside the gates looking in with the commoners I wished so hard to be.

Approaching the palace gates, I attract the attention of one of the guards; coincidentally it's Michel - the same one I instructed to open the gates that fateful night. I pray that he remembers and that he believes me.

'Michel, do you remember a few months ago when Isabella asked you to open these gates on the night there was a girl crouched down and sobbing at the gates?'

'Yes, Mademoiselle, I do remember that.' The guard looks at me rather suspiciously.

'Well, the girl who walked out of here later that night wasn't the crying girl but it was me, Princess Isabella. I am the true Princess; please can you let me in so I can be with my family? I've already missed the chance to say goodbye to my father.'

The guard surveys every inch of my face, looking for a sign of recognition. In the end he shakes his head.

'I know it's hard to believe,' I say desperately. 'I don't expect you to believe me but all I ask is that you request Isabella to come down, so she can confirm it's true. She'll be able to set this whole thing straight. Please, Michel, I am begging you.'

The guard raises his voice. 'I don't know how you found out my name, but I know who I let out that night: I will not be disturbing the royal family, especially not at a time like this. Now please go. You are becoming a nuisance.'

Walking away, I take one last look at the palace, at what used to be my home. I realise now that I may never be able to get back. Not only have I lost my father but I've lost my whole family, my destiny and everything that made me who I am. I may have achieved my freedom but at the cost of everything I ever held dear. What a fool I've been, for never realising how blessed I was. My father was right, I *was* ungrateful. I was selfish and only thinking about myself, and as with all selfish people I've ended up alone, unable to be with my family when they need me the most. I've got what I deserve and it's been the harshest lesson of my life.

As I board the train that'll take me back to Paris, I think of Sophia and wonder if she still wants me to return. I feel sad to know that we'll never meet again as I'd hoped when this was all behind us that we could all be friends. However, I do still have Mireille and for that I'm grateful.

Chapter 31

'Baptiste, what are you doing here? Why are you not in Paris?' I bump into him in the corridor, he is dressed all in black, and I'm surprised and concerned that he's here and not still looking for Isabella.

'Your Majesty, I couldn't stay in Paris once the King died because all leave is cancelled and I was required to return to Fontainebleau as soon as possible. I tried to find her, I really did, but all the leads we had came to nothing.' He lowers his voice even further. 'My dear, I shall now give you some advice: *leave the past in the past.* Your silly little game has had the most unfortunate consequences but you are to be Queen, so you need to make that your priority. This has to stop now. Isabella made her choice not to return and we've tried so hard to find her but we can't. It's clear she isn't coming back.'

'But she wouldn't do that,' I exclaim, then smile at a passing chambermaid, who curtseys. 'I know she wouldn't!' I add hotly.

'You only met her once, so let me tell you as someone who has known her all her life. This is typical of Isabella. She's reckless and most of all, I'm sad to say, she's selfish.'

I watch as Baptiste strides away, my heart heavy. Have I

in fact been deceived by Isabella? Could she really have left with no intention of coming back? Is she really so selfish that she would forsake her loving family for her freedom? While I have to admit that her behaviour does suggest that, I cannot believe it of her. It's true I only met her once but I liked her; I don't believe she would have lied.

I can't be Queen, I don't have any idea what to do. Surely, she isn't going to leave me here? There must be a part of her that wants to be Queen deep down? After all, this is her destiny not mine.

'Isabella, it's so good to see you again'. I turn to see Frederick in the lobby, his entourage bringing in his bags.

'Freddie! I had no idea you would be coming so soon. How are you?'

I race over and give him a big hug, which he returns, murmuring, 'I'm so sorry, Isabella,' and we gaze at each other for a moment before we both take a single step backwards.

'How are you feeling?' he asks tenderly. 'You must be so devastated; you were so close to your father.'

'If I'm honest, it hasn't really sunk in yet. I feel as if I'm in a dream - it doesn't feel real at all.'

'It's only natural to feel that way. You've so much going on with the funeral and Coronation, it probably won't feel real until after that.'

'How long are you staying?'

'Right up until the Coronation. It seems so long since our trip to Paris, and I've been looking forward to seeing you again, but in better circumstances, of course.'

'I have too, Freddie.' We both take a step back as Alix walks past. I notice as she subtly raises her eyebrows at me.

I bid Frederick goodbye and make my way to the kitchens

to check on the catering arrangements for the funeral with Leonda. When I walk into the kitchens, however, Leonda isn't there; instead there's a young man around my age dressed in his chef's whites who smiles at me warmly as I walk in.

'Please accept my most sincere condolences, Isabella. It's been a while since you came to speak to me,' he adds. 'I've missed our chats.'

'Excuse me? Who are you?' Baptiste hasn't mentioned him.

The young man stops what he's doing and stares at me for what seems like an age.

'I'm Eddie – Leonda's son. Do you not remember me, Isabella? How can that be?'

'Of course, I do. Sorry, Eddie, I'm just out of sorts, that's all. It's all this stress.'

I can tell from the furrow of his eyes that he isn't buying it.

'What's my surname?' he demands.

'Eddie, I don't have time for games. And you are being very rude. Now do you know where Leonda is or not!'

He looks downcast. 'I'm sorry, Isabella forgive me. I didn't mean to upset you. I was just thinking the other day about when we were children. Do you remember how we used to spend all our time catching crickets? You were so bossy, ordering me to catch them as you were too scared. You always insisted they were your favourites, because *Pinocchio* was your favourite movie, but you could never bring yourself to touch them.'

My heart begins to beat faster and I feel out of my depth, I've no choice but to go along with it.

'How sweet of you to remember. I'm sorry if you thought

that I had forgotten because I really hadn't. I smile at the young man before continuing 'It's just been such a hectic time. I hope you understand.'

'Of course I do,' he says smoothly. 'My mother has had to go and discuss the meat order with the funeral caterers, but I'll be sure to let her know that you wish to speak to her, *Your Highness*.'

'Thank you, Eddie,' I say weakly. 'I appreciate that.'

I leave the kitchens after what had begun to feel like an inquisition, sensing that I've had a narrow escape. For a moment there I thought he was trying to catch me out. Just when I think I've met everyone, someone else seems to appear out of nowhere.

I walk back to my room, fearful that this whole charade could still come crashing down. I wonder what Frederick would think of me if he knew? How disappointed he would be that I'd lied to him. Would he ever forgive me?

The day of the King's funeral arrives and thousands line the streets. I travel behind the gun carriage drawn by Navy officers along the processional route towards the railway station, and then on to the funeral train, which will take us to the Basilica St Denis, the final resting place of the Kings and Queens of France. I gaze at the mourners lining the route, trying to spot Isabella amongst them, certain that she would come to witness her father's funeral. Perhaps she will be there in Paris.

I ride in silence with the other members of the family. The crowds of people start to feel oppressive; each and every eye falls on me. My nerves jangle uncontrollably as beads of sweat start to form on my head. I've no idea what is expected of me. *I'm not supposed to be here, this isn't supposed to be me.* I feel the panic rise inside of me.

'Isabella, darling, just calm down, take deep breaths' . . . the soon to be Queen mother, squeezes my hand.

I do as I'm told and begin to feel better; my face flushing in the spring-time heat. The journey seems to take for ever, for the procession is going at a snail's pace from the Palais du Fountainebleau to the station where a train awaits us, to carry the royal casket. The gun carriage is not being pulled by car or by horse, but by foot as tradition dictates.

Finally, we all arrive at the Basilica St Denis, walking solemnly behind the coffin as the pallbearers carry it down the aisle of the grand gothic church. The arches rise majestically above our heads, while the stained-glass windows let in a colourful and beautifully refracted light.

The pallbearers walk in martial time towards the altar, lower the coffin onto the stand provided, which is draped in the royal arms, then salute and stand back. It is our turn to then bring a single blood-red rose and place it upon the King's coffin, four precious red roses against the backdrop of pure white lilies.

The service, which is recorded and relayed to people all over the world, goes by in a blur. I follow the motions as I should because in truth, my mind is not even on the funeral, but the Coronation. How will I be able to vow my allegiance to the French crown, with the eyes of the world upon me? How can I give my allegiance knowing it is all a lie? But how can I not? It's treason, years ago this would have been punishable by death. So, what will my punishment be? How will this all be resolved?

My thoughts turn to Isabella, she should be sat here with her sisters and her mother. Whatever her motives for not coming back, I pray silently that Isabella won't hate me for being where she should have been.

Chapter 32

'So, what do you want me to call you - Sophia or Isabella?' Mireille asks me. I'm back at the apartment with no idea about what happens now? What will I do for the rest of my life?

I think about it for a second. 'Well, I can't go back to my old identity now, so I suppose we'd better stick to Sophia. I'm so sorry that you've lost the real Sophia again, Mireille.' 'It is all my fault.'

'I haven't lost her at all. I know this is not the end of the story. Besides, I had to live without my sister for many years while she was away at school, and our bond did not break then, so I'm sure it will endure this time too.' Mireille is so comforting and wise. She adds kindly, 'I'm only sorry you don't have a way of getting back. I was so sure Eddie would help you, but I suppose you can't blame him for not believing you. Although he should have trusted you.'

I can tell she feels that Eddie let me down, but she's too nice to say so.

'I just wish I could have got to see Daddy one last time, but it wasn't meant to be. He would have called for me, I know he would have. And there would have been things he wanted to say but now I'll never know what they were. He will have said them to Sophia instead.' I sob, my eyes sore and red, as Mireille gently strokes my back.

'Do you not think it might have helped if you had stood in the crowd yesterday? At least you could have felt a little part of funeral and had the chance to say goodbye.'

I sigh. 'No, that's just ceremonial and I hate all that rubbish. That's exactly what I wanted to get away from. Nothing can bring back the time I should have had with Daddy. It's my own fault. I've hurt so many people by being selfish. Eddie told me chasing my freedom was a bad idea but I didn't listen. Why am I always so stubborn?'

Before Mireille can respond, the doorbell rings, making us both jump. I'm in too much of a state to answer it.

'Mireille, will you go? I'm afraid it might be Yvette and Marcel, come to find out if everything is all right. I just can't face them right now.'

I go to hide myself in my room, hoping that the De Castellanes won't come in. However, a few moments later there's a knock at my door. I pull the duvet over me and try to pretend that I am sleeping, but then I hear the door open and two sets of footsteps enter my room.

'Sophia, you have a visitor, I think you'll want to see him.'

I throw my bedcovers off and see Eddie standing beside Mireille in my room. He smiles at me sheepishly as I get out of bed and stand up straight in front of him, folding my arms across my chest.

'What do you want, Eddie?' I know I look a sight, with my make-up washed off and my bloodshot eyes. But I don't care.

'I just want you to know that I do believe you're Isabella. Of course, you weren't lying and I'm sorry.'

'What's made you change your mind?' I ask. 'Now it's too late, I may add. You made it perfectly clear the last time we spoke that you didn't believe me - so forgive me if I question why the sudden change of heart.' I know I sound sarcastic but to my mind it's the least he deserves.

'It's a couple of things,' he explains humbly. 'Firstly, before you left you shouted at me that you would sack both myself and my mother. I've never told you my mother worked at the palace. Also, when I returned there for the King's funeral, the Isabella I thought was you came into the kitchens and didn't even know who I was. When I told her we were old friends, she pretended to recognise me so I asked her my surname but she got cross. I changed tactics and told her about my fondest memory of our childhood, when we used to chase crickets with our nets and how they were her favourite insect when she was growing up.'

Despite myself, I shudder. 'Crickets - are you serious? I hated them. We caught butterflies, not crickets.'

'She didn't know that. The Isabella I thought was you had no idea about it. As soon as I realised the truth, I came straight back to find you, to help you get back to the palace. I know it's too late for you to see your father, and I'm so sorry about that, but it's not too late for your Coronation. Come - get yourself ready. Time is short and we need to leave now.'

'I'm so pleased that you'll finally get to return home.' Mireille encloses me in her arms, and says emotionally, 'I'll never forget all that you've done for me or the fun times we've had together.'

'What are you talking about, Mireille? You're coming with us. Grab your things - we have a train to catch. Eddie, how long do we have?' My anger subsides now I have the chance to get home. This is my opportunity to reclaim my family and my own identity - and I shall seize it with both hands.

'The Coronation ceremony starts at 11 a.m. It's now 9 a.m. so we have two hours. You need to get ready as soon as possible. It takes two hours to get there and we will need to change at Gare De Lyon for the Light Railway. We can't get a taxi as the roads will be impassable, they'll be no chance of getting near it.'

Mireille and I dash around, cleaning our teeth, dragging a comb through our hair, putting on a tiny amount of make-up and throwing on the closest outfit that comes to hand. In little over ten minutes, we have locked up the flat and are on the way to the train station to get to the Basilica St Denis, the same cathedral where my father was buried only yesterday.

Arriving at the station we have a short wait until the next train arrives at 10am. On the screens they are playing footage of the Coronation, I watch as Sophia emerges from the palace, I see the fear in her eyes as she waves to the crowds. Frederick steps forward to help her into the ceremonial carriage before kissing her hand and departing. As I watch Sophia and Frederick, the words of the newspaper-seller come to mind: they do look like a couple. It's clear that they have fallen for each other.

'Is that really my sister?' I hear Mireille whisper to herself.

'Yes, it really is. She's such a natural; she's better at this than me.'

'I would be inclined to agree with you there,' Eddie jokes. 'You never were a typical Princess, were you?'

'Hey Eddie, you're not supposed to agree with me but yes, I know what you mean. I was too independent to be an obedient royal.'

The train finally pulls into the station, every second the train sits at the station feels like an hour. As the train pulls away towards Paris, my nerves start to kick in. What if nobody believes me? What if they think I'm just insane? I raise my hand to my throat - and feel the locket Daddy made for me against my skin.

Arriving at Gare De Lyon it is now 11.05am. We make our way to catch the second train that will take us to the Basilica St Denis, luckily the train is there when we get to the platform and we run to ensure we all catch it. The train is packed but we manage to wedge ourselves on, nothing is stopping me from getting this train.

It's just gone 11.30am when the train pulls in to the Basilica St Denis station. The Coronation has begun and there are hundreds of people in our way. We still have a 20-minute journey by foot but with the amount of people it could take even longer.

'Let's hold on so we don't lose each other in the crowds,' I gasp. 'There's no way to do this but barge our way through.'

As we shove past them, angry people protest but it doesn't stop us and we finally wrestle out way through and arrive at the barrier surrounding the building at 12.05pm. I quickly try to climb over but a guard immediately approaches, his face angry.

'Stop that, mademoiselle. This barrier is there for a reason,' he says sternly.

'Are you permitted to enter?' says another one of the guards, addressing Eddie.

'Yes, they are both with me, I'm Eddie Laurent, I'm on the list.'

We watch as the guardsman consults the list. It seems

to take forever – suddenly I hear the rousing sound of the choir and instantly know that the crowning is about to take place at any moment.

'Yes, so you are. Really sir, you're not allowed to take in two guests.'

'I grew up at the palace and this is my girlfriend Sophia and this lady is the Queen's best friend from school. The whole reason we're late is that I was tasked to find her. I know, it was very last-minute but the Queen has been so upset about her father I wanted to surprise her.'

The guard quickly pats us down, then he nods.

'Very well. I'll let you in but keep your heads down. Quick - or you'll miss it.'

'Thank you so much, we appreciate it.'

As the mighty doors creak open, I can hear the final incantations being spoken and I see the crown poised to be placed upon Sophia's bent head. Her anguished expression visible. Watching, I see the crown being placed gently upon Sophia's head.

'*Stop the Coronation!* That's not the Queen, stop the Coronation!' Leaving both Eddie and Mireille behind, I race as fast as I can down the aisle - but before I can reach the altar I'm thrown to the ground by armed protection officers. I feel one press his gun against my head, but I still try to scream to stop.

'Let her speak!' It's Sophia's voice.

The armed officer removes the gun from my head and lifts me up, frisking me for any concealed weapons before marching me down to the front of the altar.

'This is not Queen Isabella. She is called Sophia Lazarus and we switched places. It isn't her fault, I asked her to but I am the true Princess Isabella, not the person you are crowning as the Queen of France.'

There's a stunned silence throughout the whole cathedral.

Sophia's voice is clear and it rings throughout the ancient building.

'It's the truth. That is the real Princess Isabella and I am Sophia Lazarus. We did change places in the strangest story ever told - but I couldn't tell anyone as it would have put your future Queen at risk. I had to carry on pretending to be her until she was able to return. Come here Isabella' I go to join Sophia at the altar, she smiles warmly as I approach her.

The Bishop asks me: 'Do you have any proof that you are Isabella of the House of Bourbon?'

I unfasten the locket from around my neck, and pass it to the Bishop 'This is the locket my father gave me for my eighteenth birthday. Ask my mother to verify that it is the correct one.'

The Bishop collects the necklace from me and takes it over to my mother, who is sat in the front of the Cathedral, looking as confused as everyone else. She takes the locket in her hand and examines it before rising from her seat and coming over to me and Sophia.

'Yes, this is the locket that Isabella was given by the King for her eighteenth birthday - but how can there be two? I've seen my daughter wearing it.'

Sophia raises her hand to her neck to reveal the necklace that she has been wearing, which is indeed a locket but with no sapphires on it.

'I also got this locket on my eighteenth birthday, but it was from my best friend at school and it isn't the same at all. Please, see the for yourself.'

Looking at us both, my mother cries: 'How could I not

have known? What kind of mother am I, if I can't even tell my own daughter from a complete stranger? How did this happen?'

'I'm sorry, Mama,' I say.

Taking my mother by the hand, I say: 'Do you remember the night you came to my room and found me with Sophia? You made me make her leave, but before you and Daddy had come into the room, we had switched clothes and done our hair the same - so when you thought it was Sophia who left the palace that night, it was in fact me.'

'Oh Isabella, how could you have done that? Where have you been all this time?' She clings to me, then grabs Sophia by the hand too.

'I've been in Paris, Mama. I've had a job, like an ordinary citizen. Oh Mama, I've learned so much and I've changed so much too.' I hold her close and weep. 'I'm so sorry, Mama, I tried to get back before Daddy died but no one would believe me. No one would let me near any of you. I'll regret it for the rest of my life. If only I could have seen him one last time. I know I've been so selfish. I'm so sorry, please forgive me.'

While the Queen holds us both, Sophia speaks again.

'I tried to find you, Isabella. I sent someone to look for you in Paris but we had no clues to follow. I know it's not much, but everything your father said to me, I've written down for you. Those words were meant for you - and it broke my heart to think that you wouldn't hear them.' Turning to my mother she continues 'Your majesty, I am so sorry too. I hope you can understand why I couldn't say anything, as the days went on it just got worse and worse and I just didn't know what to do. I didn't want Isabella to be in any danger'.

I see my mother smile at Sophia and give her a big hug, as she wipes the tears from her eyes.

I reply 'Oh Sophia, you don't know what it'll mean to read those words and to know what my father wanted to say to me. I'm so sorry, I didn't mean for any of this to happen. I'm so sorry I couldn't get back before now. I'll protect you, I'll make sure no-one blames you for any of this. I promise you.'

'You're back now, that's the main thing. This is your destiny, not mine, and here - this belongs to you.' Sophia raises her hands above her head and lifts off the heavy gold crown where she attempts to place it upon my head.

'If you don't mind, young lady, that is my job,' the Bishop says with a smile, taking it away from her and placing it back on the velvet cushion.

Finally, I take my rightful place upon the throne, the ceremonial robe draped over the clothes I arrived in.

Sophia joins my mother and sisters at the front of the cathedral, while Eddie and Mireille are placed behind them, next to Prince Frederick and the Swiss royal family.

Seated upon the throne as the Coronation is completed, I can almost feel my father stood beside me, his hand on my shoulder, encouraging me. I can picture the pride on his face as I finally face my destiny: to be Queen of France.

The Pretender

Chapter 33

As I awake the morning after the Coronation, I find myself brooding about Freddie. While it's a massive relief not to have to pretend to be someone else, to have everything out in the open. I've no idea what to do with my life now that he won't be in it.

'Sophia, are you awake?' The bedroom door opens and Isabella comes into my room, plonking herself on to my bed. 'I just wanted to speak to you properly after all the commotion yesterday. The thing is, I'd really like it if you could stay here for a while until all the media interest dies down. I know the press will hound you relentlessly. So, will you and Mireille please stay here with me, for now at least?'

'Are you sure? I don't want to intrude, I'm sure we'd be fine.'

'Have you seen the crowds outside the gates? You would be mobbed. Having you here, with Mireille, would be so lovely. We'll all be together. I'd really like that.' She giggles. 'As your Queen, I command you to obey.'

'Oh, all right,' I say with a distinct lack of humility. 'Now will you tell me how on earth my sister ended up in Paris with you? I was so surprised to see you both there together. I've never seen her look so happy. Thank you so much for making that happen.'

Isabella tells me the whole story and I listen, transfixed. When she finishes, she says: 'There's one thing I need to tell you though, and I hope you're not mad at me. We didn't have any money and so I had to pawn your phone to get us to Paris. I'm sorry, I'll buy you another one, I promise. I kept the SIM card for you.'

'Oh, don't be silly. I'm just glad it was you and not my father. If he had found it he would have sold it for drugs.'

She looks at me shyly. 'So, you'll stay here then for a bit? You can keep my room, I know you like it.'

'Yes, of course I'll stay. And while I do love your room, I love your family much more. So, I don't care where I sleep.'

'Now, if you get yourself ready and looking beautiful, would you care to join me in the Blue Dining Room for lunch? It'll be my first lunch as Queen, so I'd love you to be there. Put on something nice, won't you? It's a special occasion.'

'Oh – wait. I don't have any of my own clothes. I've been wearing yours.'

'What's mine is yours. You and Mireille must take anything out of my closet that you like. By the way, I really loved your clothes. Your sister said you designed and made them yourself.'

'Yes, I made all my own clothes before I came here. It was mostly out of necessity but I really enjoyed doing it.'

'You've so much talent, Sophia. Would you make me a dress for my first state visit as Queen? I'd really like it if you could.'

'Of course, I'd be honoured to.'

I say goodbye to Isabella and jump in the shower to freshen up. While drying and styling my hair, I pick out a classic black dress from Isabella's wardrobe which I team with orange accessories so I'm able to look demure but also maintain a bit of individuality too.

Making my way down to the Blue Dining Room, I'm excited to see Mireille again. It seems like such a long time since I saw my big sister properly and I've really missed her. But when I open the doors of the dining room and walk through, I'm surprised to find it completely empty. I must be early. Approaching the table, I see that there are some place-settings right at the far end. Before I can go and find out who they are for, however, I hear the doors open behind me.

Frederick enters the room. 'Hello, Sophia Lazarus,' he says. 'I don't believe that we've met before?'

For a moment, I don't know what to do. I feel weak and clutch the table before sitting down on a nearby chair.

'I was supposed to go home straight after the Coronation,' he tells me, 'but Isabella took me aside and asked me to stay. She said she wanted to speak to me last night.'

'Really?' I seem to have lost my voice.

'Yes. She wanted to explain what had happened - wanted me to understand the predicament you had been put into, through no fault of your own. How she had been supposed to return after one week but let you down. I think she wanted to make sure I knew just how capable you were in the role of a royal.'

'I don't see the difference that would make,' I manage to say but it comes out as a squeak.

'Do you not, Sophia? Do you really not see the difference it makes?'

His voice sounds tender but I'm confused, shouldn't he be angry?

'Frederick - Freddie - you have every reason to be mad at me because I wasn't honest with you. I fully understand that you can't stand by the feelings you had in Paris, but I just want you to know that I couldn't say anything, however much I may have wanted to, because if it had become common knowledge, Isabella would have been out there unprotected and in danger. I couldn't let that happen - but that's the only reason I lied to you. Can you forgive me?'

'There's nothing for me to forgive - and I'm certainly not angry. I'm impressed at how expertly you undertook all those duties. Isabella and I have spent our lives being trained but you had nothing and yet you did so well. I'm sorry I did not make myself clearer. Sophia darling, Isabella wanted me to know what a fantastic Queen you would make.'

He takes my hand and says: 'Sophia Lazarus, you may be a commoner and an unwilling Pretender to the throne but I fell in love with you in Paris and I'm pretty sure that you fell in love with me too. However, there was a big problem with this when I thought you were Isabella, because as heirs to two different thrones, one of us would have to abdicate. I knew that if I ever abdicated, my father would never speak to me again; I would never again be permitted to see any of my family. So, as you can see, there were real difficulties with me thinking I was in love with Isabella.'

'I fell in love with you too, Freddie, how could I not? You're everything I've ever wanted in a guy and so much more. Even if you weren't a Prince, I'd have loved you anyway. But I'm not an aristocrat, I'm a pauper Freddie and I know this changes this things for us.'

'Not to me it doesn't, my feelings remain the same as they were in Paris. It's a better situation because I can one day succeed to the Swiss throne with no need to abdicate. Now let me speak the truth, Sophia. Your background is not ideal but it's not a problem either. The Swiss press will love you because you're not a Princess. You are one of them and that is always appealing to the public. All the things that you think keep us apart are in your head.'

He stops speaking and clears his throat. He seems nervous.

'I delayed my flight because I wanted to ask you a question.'

Freddie moves towards me, taking my hands and lifting me up from my chair.

'Sophia, how would you feel about moving to Geneva? How would you feel about being my girlfriend?'

I hear the words and also hear the love in them. My heart soars.

'Yes, Freddie, I'd love to move to Switzerland with you and I'd love to be your girlfriend.'

'So, when I leave for home, shall we leave together?'

'Don't you need to ask permission first?'

'I already have. My father gives his blessing, he also thinks you'll make a great royal.'

'In that case, the answer is yes, Your Royal Highness. A thousand times yes!'

Chapter 34

Ten years later . . .

The sound of my baby's cry rouses me from my sleep. I walk over to her crib at the end of our bed, pick her up and comfort her. As I look down at her rosebud face, I feel so grateful that she is mine. Never would I have believed how much I could love another person as much as I love my husband.

'Good morning, darling, do you want me to change her nappy? You've got a long day today.'

'No, don't worry, Eddie, I'm awake anyway. You go back to sleep.'

As I feed Anastasia, I watch the shadowed hills in the distance. With the darkness giving way to the light, I think about my father. In my heart, I know that he'd be proud of me, not only as a Queen but as a mother. I wish with all my heart that he could be here today, to meet my very own Princess, his granddaughter.

I recall those long-ago days in Paris, the simple fun I had with Mireille and my first date with Eddie. Little did I realise he would become my husband, my best friend and my Prince. Finally, I think of Sophia, of the events that changed both of our lives for ever. Neither of us could have foreseen the ramifications of that night, of the bold decision we took. While it did bring its share of regrets, it's also brought us both a great deal of happiness. We will always be grateful to each other.

'Your Highness, shall I take Anastasia? We need to get you dressed and ready.'

I hand my baby daughter over to her nanny while my hairdresser styles my hair and my dresser helps me put on my beautiful outfit. I stand before the mirror in a baby-blue fitted dress with delicate chiffon sleeves and silver embroidery giving it a wonderful shimmer. The hairdresser moves in to team it with a silver fascinator to complete the look.

Eddie and I walk to the waiting car, where we're joined by mama, my two sisters and their respective boyfriends. We all get into our cars and are driven to the outskirts of Paris, to the Basilica St Denis.

As ever, a crowd awaits us, and the mood is joyful. I wanted to have my daughter christened in this sacred place. I think of all the memories this building holds for me. It is here that I was crowned Queen. It was here that I married my beloved husband and it is here that my father's remains lie. Whenever I'm here, I feel especially close to him. I nervously touch my locket, then the ring he bequeathed to me - the ring that his father gave to him - and I feel his presence, just like he said I would.

As I reach the altar, I smile warmly at the friends who are already gathered there waiting for us.

'Mireille, it's so good to see you. How are you?'

'I'm fine, thank you, it's so good to see you too, Isabella. Oh, look how much Anastasia has grown! She looks so much like you.'

'Your Royal Highness, the Queen of Switzerland!' I say, greeting Sophia with a grin. 'So glad you could make it today.'

'Isabella, will you stop doing that. You know I don't like you calling me that.' Sophia embraces my mother and sisters.

'I know,' I admit. 'That's why I keep doing it. It's so good to see you, I've missed you.'

'I've missed you too.' She looks around. 'It's always so strange to come back here and not think about the Coronation Day . . . To think I nearly became the Queen of France. Phew! Who knew how much our lives would change from that point on.'

'I know - I remember you standing there and telling me that this was *my* destiny not yours, but the irony is that it was *both* our destinies, when I realised you were destined to be Queen, just as much as I was. Then this whole situation suddenly made sense.'

Sophia reaches out to gently tickle Anastasia's tiny cheek. 'I wouldn't go that far,' she says. 'I'm not sure any of it makes sense.'

'So, when's the baby due? I can't believe how big you've got.'

'I've got two months left. It's getting scary now but I don't think it's possible for me to get any bigger. Beautiful dress, by the way. Who made it for you?'

'Funny you should ask. It's a small design house that's grown very large over the past few years, isn't that right, Mireille?'

She nods. 'Yes, I finally managed to put my business degree to good use and now I run a very successful fashion company - but the identity of the designer is the best-kept secret in the business. Nobody knows who's behind the designs so beloved by the Queens of France and Switzerland.'

'Well, Mireille, that's not strictly true. We know exactly who it is, don't we, Sophia?'

'Yes, we do, but it must remain our secret. It's the perfect hobby for me while I'm travelling and besides, Mireille truly is the brains behind the business. I just provide the designs.'

We all take our seats together as the christening starts. Eddie is beside me, and my mama and my sisters are close at hand. Finally, I look over to where my father lies and feel that in this moment, everyone dear to me is under one roof, just as it's supposed to be.

The priest calls upon the godmothers and the godfather of the child to step forward. Sophia, Mireille and Freddie join me, Eddie and Anastasia at the font where she is baptised with holy water and christened. A tear comes to my eye as I think back to the day I met Sophia, the bruised and beaten girl I stumbled upon at the palace gates and how she and Mireille came to be as dear to me as my own family. It was after the death of their parents some years ago, that I got to meet Manon. Slowly they have begun to reconcile their differences. How proud we all felt when she said she wanted to train to be a solicitor, to help protect children in similar situations to theirs growing up.

Ever since I can remember, my father always spoke to me about my destiny to be Queen. I used to roll my eyes and try to change the subject. It felt as if my destiny was on a plate, and all I needed to do was take it - but that wasn't true. In order to fulfil that destiny, I had to help

Sophia fulfil hers too. Our destinies were intertwined with one another's, like a golden thread, weaving two strangers together in inexplicable ways.

Whoever would have thought that as a Princess and a Pretender, we would share the same destiny, to become Queen.

The End

Acknowledgements

I would like to extend a special thank you to all the people who worked alongside me and whose support and expertise has helped make my dream a reality. These special people are:

Joan Deitch for providing such wonderful editorial support and guidance.

Emma Haines for her beautiful illustrations that have helped bring my story to life.

Ollie Eskriett for taking all the above elements and turning it into an incredible reality.

Nicola May for offering her support and guidance on the self-publishing process.

You have all been amazing and I've really enjoyed working with you all on my novel.

If you have enjoyed reading *'The Pretender'* would you please consider writing a review on one of the many review platforms available, so others who would enjoy this story are also able to discover my work.

Printed in Great Britain
by Amazon